WAR ON THE RIDGE

"I see one of the bastards, up on the ridge!" Pepe gasped and dashed forward to scale the black rocks behind the seated lookout.

The lookout didn't stay seated the other way long, as he heard Pepe scrambling up to join him. He pivoted on one buttock and blew Pepe away with the rifle held across his thighs. Then he got blown off the far side of the ridge as Captain Gringo, cursing them both, charged forward with the Maxim braced on one hip, spitting lead!

Gringo took the same route up the steep rocky slope, then ran along the ridge with the machine-gun belt lashing behind him like the tail of an angry cat—as he fired short but deadly bursts at anyone who wanted to argue about it!

Novels by
Ramsay Thorne

Published by
WARNER BOOKS

Renegade #26

BLOOD ON THE BORDER

Ramsay Thorne

WARNER BOOKS

A Warner Communications Company

WARNER BOOKS EDITION

Warner Books, Inc.
666 Fifth Avenue
New York, N.Y. 10103

 A Warner Communications Company

Printed in the United States of America

First Printing: September, 1984

10 9 8 7 6 5 4 3 2 1

The talk was getting tense two tables to Captain Gringo's left. But so far neither of the tough-looking Costa Ricans sharing the canopy of the sidewalk cantina with him had gotten to "tu madre!" yet. And meanwhile, a bouncy brunette named Bianca had just promised to meet the tall American there at sunset, weather and her sometimes-indulgent dueña permitting. So Captain Gringo simply placed the correct change for his cerveza on the tin table in case he had to beat a hasty exit and hoped for the best.

The sinking sun was casting a ruddy blush on the stucco saints of the old Spanish baroque cathedral across the plaza, and the nightly paseo would soon be starting. Hopefully, the two guys growling at each other next door were just joshing to kill time as they waited for the dames to show up.

They weren't. When the big blond Yanqui heard somebody gasp and then shout, "You mention my mother? You dare?" he rose quietly and was well on his way before he heard the dulcet tones of breaking glass behind him as someone added, "Go home and *fuck* your mother if you are so fond of her, you sucker of cocks for centavos!"

Captain Gringo didn't linger to hear the answer as he ducked around the first corner he came to. But it sounded like a .32 Short, as near as he could judge at this life-preserving distance.

A muchacha wearing a red flamenco dress was heading toward the cantina on the narrow walk ahead of him, which was definitely going in the wrong direction. So Captain Gringo grabbed her, tossed her over his shoulder, and started running as, around the corner, a no-nonsense .44-40 proceeded to clear its throat with monotonous regularity. The muchacha he'd snatched on the fly seemed confused, for some reason. She kept hammering his back with her little balled-up fists as she protested, "Por favor,

1

Señor! How dare you carry me like a banana bunch? And to where, and for why?''

Captain Gringo didn't slow down as he told her she was too pretty to die. Meanwhile, a voice behind them was telling the whole world to call la policía and might have yelled more had it not ended in another gunshot and a scream of agony.

By now Captain Gringo had made it to the shoulder-high stretch of garden wall he'd hoped might still be where he remembered. So, as tin police whistles chirped like bewildered birds all around and more gunshots echoed from the plaza behind them, he tossed the muchacha over the wall and vaulted it after her, blindly.

It worked out all right for both of them. As he'd recalled, the long-abandoned garden behind the wall had gone to a cushion of tall grass and minty herbs, providing a reasonably soft landing place for falling bodies. But apparently his newfound comrade in arms hadn't done this sort of thing as often as the muscular soldier of fortune had. For when Captain Gringo sat up, the muchacha was still sprawled like a rag doll, face down, at the base of the single old mimosa tree shading the little weed patch.

Captain Gringo crawled to the girl and rolled her over to see if she was really hurt. Her big hazel eyes stared owlishly up at him as she pleaded in a confused tone, ''Jesus, Maria, y José! Would someone tell me in a more simpatico fashion what the fuck is going on?''

He chuckled, then winced as a wild round ticked through the mimosa leaves above them. He sighed and said, ''It's a 'tu madre' in the plaza, if only it would *stay* in the plaza! La policía figure to start grabbing every ass in sight. But I think we're safe here, for now. How are you called, Señorita?''

She shook her head and replied, ''What kind of a muchacha do you think I am, Señor? The paseo has not even *started,* and I never give my name to any hombre before we have smiled at one another in passing at least a dozen times. You are an Anglo, no?''

He nodded but said, "I know how the paseo works. It figures to start a little late this evening." Then he tossed his planter's hat on the weeds, took off his linen jacket, and made a pillow of it for her head as he added, "We're going to have to stay put for a spell. The natives seem restless tonight."

She stared thoughtfully at the now-exposed shoulder rig holding his double-action .38 against his left ribs and asked, "Are you a dangerous person, Señor Americano?"

He laughed and propped himself on one elbow in the weeds at her side before he said, "Not very dangerous. I hardly ever eat pretty little muchachas."

"Oh? Not even if you like them very much?"

He took a slow look around as he digested her double meaning. The mimosa screened them pretty well from the few small windows he could see overlooking them from the surrounding houses, and it was getting darker by the minute. On the other hand, she looked a little young as well as fresh lipped, and the noises from the other side of the wall had subsided to mere dramatic shouting. So he said, "It should be safe to boost you back over the wall in a few minutes, Worldly Woman of Mystery."

She dimpled up at him, her soft black hair spread to frame her pretty oval face as she asked, "And where will *you* be going then? The paseo, for to see if you can discover my name?"

He repressed a grimace as he replied, "You'll no doubt drive the men wild by lamplight. I'm going back to my own quarters, via that *other* wall across the way and an alley I can take through the block. I had some more attractive plans for later this evening, but now . . ."

"More attractive plans than *me?*" she cut in with a hurt look.

So he assured her, "Nobody in San José is more attractive than you and you know it. What I meant was that la policía make me nervioso, and for some reason hombres like me make la policía nervioso too, when things get noisy."

She regarded his blond Anglo-Saxon features thoughtfully as she asked, "Oh? Are you wanted by the law, Yanqui?"

He shook his head and said, "Not here in Costa Rica, at the moment. I want to keep it that way if I possibly can. So I'd best skip the paseo, if they have one tonight, and settle for going to bed with a good book." Then he couldn't help adding, "Unless you have a better suggestion."

She didn't answer. But the smoke signals she was sending up at him from those smoldering eyes had to mean *something*. So he bent down to kiss her, and she kissed back with an obviously experienced as well as teasing tongue. But when he tried to determine if either of those yummy bulges in her red bodice was real, she pushed him away and protested, "Stop that! What kind of a muchacha do you take me for!"

He didn't tell her. It was impolite to call a lady a prick tease. He said, "Sorry. Your ravishing beauty simply made me lose my head for a moment. We'd better get you back over the wall before I get carried away by your utterly *un*earthly charms again."

She didn't get it. But he didn't care, and he'd meant the part about getting her out of his hair. Life was too short, even for a man without a price on his head, to waste this much of it on a tease.

But then some other bitch with a much uglier voice called out from somewhere above them in the gathering dusk, "I see you down there under that mimosa, Maria Castro! I see you like a puta in the grass with that hombre!"

Captain Gringo made a wry face as he finally spotted the outline of the old battle-ax in a distant window and said, "She's got good eyes. Is she anyone we really have to worry about, Maria?"

The girl beside him under the mimosa laughed and replied, "Not really. For one thing, I am not Maria Castro. But I *know* the stuck-up little snip, and, sí, come to think of it she does have a dress like this one and . . . Oh, this is most delicioso! Would you kiss me again, por favor?''

He frowned thoughtfully and said, ''I don't think I'd better. I don't have anything against that other muchacha, and we already seem to have her in trouble.''

But the girl who was *not* Maria Castro reached up to pull him down atop her as the old bat watching gasped and said, ''Ay, que muchacha! Wait until I tell your madre about this, you wicked child!''

Captain Gringo kissed back. Any normal man would have. But when they came up for air he protested, ''Listen, this is a pretty shitty trick to play on the innocent lady, Doll!''

But the mystery muchacha in his arms hissed, ''I know! I owe her for similar favors in the past! You see, that old hag spying on us is not the first to notice we look much alike at a distance!''

He knew she was right when their distant tormentor shouted, ''Don't think I can't see what you two are up to down there, Maria Castro! It is not that dark, and that mimosa does not hide your wicked ways as you might think! As for you, you wicked hombre in those khaki pants, I can see every move you make with her, and I warn you, Maria is only sixteen and still a virgin!''

He muttered, ''Jesus!'' as the young girl laughed and said, ''A lot *she* knows! I wonder who she is. She certainly does not know our Maria as well as we do, eh?''

''I don't know her at all, and this is still a dirty trick, damm it!'' Then he gasped and added, ''Jesus H. Christ, let go of my fly! I don't play kid games, *with* kids or *on* kids, and . . .''

But she wasn't playing kid games, although her game was going from just plain dirty to vicious as the old woman watching screamed, ''Ay, Maria Mala! You shall surely roast in hell forever!'' Captain Gringo told her to for God's sake stop. But his heart wasn't really in it once she had his raging erection in her mouth, so he added,

"Hey, watch those fucking *teeth!*" as she proceeded to fuck him with her bobbing head!

His enjoyment was somewhat marred by the hag shouting, "Francisco! Come here and see what Maria Castro is doing *now!* She is even worse than they say in the mercado de hortalizas!"

Captain Gringo swore, shoved the mystery muchacha's head from his lap, and rolled her on her back to mount her right as she protested, "Oh, what do you think you are *doing,* Señor?"

It was a stupid question. But he growled, "The best I *can* do for poor Maria Castro on such short notice. You know I can't stop *completely* now!"

As he shoved her red ruffles up around her hips and spread her naked tawny thighs, she protested, "Oh, no! I never go all the way on a first date, Señor!"

Then, as he proved her wrong, she clamped down on his questing shaft with her warm wet interior and added, "Oh, well, as long as Maria gets credit for this."

So they were going at it hot and heavy when they heard a weary male voice call out, "You need glasses, you silly old woman. They are sinning in a perfectly proper manner as far as I can tell from here." Then he added in a louder voice, "Hey, you kids down there, cut that out before I have la policía on you! You are driving my old woman crazy, and *I* don't like cats, dogs, or children rutting under my window, either!"

They heard window shutters slamming shut. Captain Gringo stroked her vigorously, hitting bottom on every beat, trying to put himself over the edge as soon as possible. That was easy with her tight young box, and in no time he was shooting a hot load into the little minx. After he had finished coming in her, he sighed and said, "We'd better get out of here. He might mean what he said. Your place or mine, Querida?"

"Idioto! I live with my parents, and only wicked muchachas go to a man's room with him, no?"

"Yeah, stupid questions do deserve stupid answers," he

replied, rolling off to button up and get to his feet for a discreet peek over the wall. The coast was clear. The side street was dark as well as empty at the moment. So he put on his hat and jacket, then helped her to her feet. She said, "Maybe, if we got to know one another better at the paseo . . ." and he said, "Right, I'll keep an eye out for that red dress. Upsy daisy." Then, as soon as he'd dropped her over the wall, he turned and beelined back across the garden to vault the far wall into the alley beyond.

He cut through the block without incident, walked across the street on the far side, and climbed the wooden outside stairway to the rented quarters he shared with his sidekick, Gaston Verrier, late of the French foreign legion.

His older and much smaller fellow soldier of fortune was seated at a table, cleaning his own .38 by the light of an old oil lamp that needed a good cleaning, too. Gaston looked up to ask with a sardonic smile, "Why the expression of total disgust, Dick? Are you coming down with something?"

Captain Gringo said, "Must have been something I didn't eat, thank God. What's with the gun kit?"

"Merde alors, when one fires a gun one must clean it afterwards, non? On my way home across the plaza a few minutes ago I found myself in the middle of a gunfight, for some reason."

"I heard about that gunfight. Who the hell were *you* shooting at, Gaston?"

"Anyone pointing a gun in my direction, of course. I tried not to kill anyone, since we are running out of countries without extradition treaties. How did *you* make out in the riot, my adorable child?"

Captain Gringo laughed and said, "If I told you, you'd never believe me. I hope we've got some grub in the joint. Might not be a good idea for either of us to go out again for a while."

Gaston frowned, shook his head, and said, "Mais non, Dick. As soon as I get this stubborn species of weapon back together, we have to go see Colonel Vegas, of the Costa Rican national guard. He has a job for us.''

Captain Gringo took a seat across from the drab but dapper little Frenchman and said, ''No, he hasn't. I thought we'd agreed to stay out of the local politics here in Costa Rica. So far, it's the only Central American country we haven't made enemies in. I'm sure they can manage the coup, revolt, or whatever without us, Gaston.''

The old legion deserter held his reassembled weapon up to the light, dry-fired it, and said, ''Eh bien. The colonel does not want to change the status quo, Dick. Apparently Costa Ricans like the way things are here as much as we do. The problem is along the southern border of this adorable little republic. As you know, having thrown some of the eggs into the Panama fan yourself, all hell has broken loose down that way, and all sorts of sinister people, from pure bandits to no-doubt-sincere Panamanian rebels, seem to be moving this way, with the Colombian army in hot pursuit! Colonel Vegas simply wishes to ensure that neither armed refugees nor the even more dangerous Colombian army invades Costa Rica.''

''That sounds reasonable. But where do *we* come in, Gaston? Last time I looked, Costa Rica had a pretty good little national guard of its own.''

Gaston grimaced and said, ''Merde alors, he answers his own questions and still requires parental guidance? You just said the key words, my old and dense. Costa Rica's armed forces are indeed très little and 'pretty good' is not enough to stop the heavily armed and well-trained Colombian army we have brushed with in the past, to our sorrow!''

''Okay, so why can't Costa Rica call on Tío Sam for help? Everyone knows the States have friendly relations with Costa Rica and would love a chance to clobber Colombia this season. Hell, the U.S. State Department is behind most of the revolutions in the proposed canal zone down that way. One cable to Washington would have the gunboats here in no time!''

Gaston nodded but said, ''Oui, that is just what the

Costa Ricans très desperately wish to avoid. At the moment they owe Tío Sam nothing but common courtesy. Once U.S. Marines find themselves stationed on Costa Rican soil, who can say when they might leave, or what sort of treaties Washington might press Costa Rica for, as long as they're here, hein?''

"Oh, come on, Gaston. I haven't been much of a fan of Washington since the Tenth Cav framed me on that bum rap and I had to run for my ass. But fair is fair. Us Yanks haven't grabbed any Spanish-speaking territory since back in forty-eight, and, shit, we *offered to pay* Mexico for Texas and such.''

Gaston raised an eyebrow and replied, "Perhaps Hispanics are simply suspicious by nature. I'm sure your country has their best interests in mind regarding the proposed Panama Canal, and no doubt the Cubans will be happier once Washington and M'sieur Hearst liberate them from Spain. Meanwhile, Costa Rica reserves the stubborn right to defend its own borders against all comers. So that is where you and I come in, hein?''

Captain Gringo pursed his lips and asked, "What's the colonel's deal, officers' commissions for us if we show the muchachos how it's done?''

"Mais non; as the colonel explained earlier, once Costa Rica took formal notice of our being here at all, they would have to answer all those très fatigué questions about our whereabouts from other governments less fond of us. They want us to lead a guerrilla of fellow rogues in an informal attempt to convince one and all that jumping the Costa Rican border could be injurious to one's health. Aside from the usual front money, we shall get a thousand a month plus expenses, and all the weaponry and supplies we may require. I told Vegas you preferred the Maxim machine gun to other current brands on the market, and, merde alors, Dick, you know as well as I how a soldier-of-fortune contract reads, non?''

Captain Gringo took out a Havana claro, lit it, and shook out the match before he said, "I dunno, Gaston. If we took this particular job and fucked up, where would we be able to hole up this well between jobs?''

Before Gaston could answer, they heard a dreadful commotion on the street outside. So, by unspoken agreement, they got up and moved to a front window to see what all the fuss was about.

The fuss was taking place under a streetlamp, where a burly man of about fifty was waving one arm wildly as he held a girl in a red dress with his other hand, roaring to any and all within earshot, ''By the balls of Santiago, I know that big gringo lives *somewhere* on this block, and I mean to have his severed cock on the pavement before I leave!''

Gaston asked, ''Are they anyone we know, Dick?''

Captain Gringo answered, ''Not really. But that poor little bimbo in the red dress looks something like someone else I met earlier this evening. We'd better go down the back stairs on our way to meet your pal Vegas.''

Colonel Roberto Vegas was called Bob by his English-speaking social equals, spoke English as well as they did, and looked more like an American's preconception of an English country squire than a banana-republic warlord. Like most Costa Ricans Captain Gringo had met, until recently, the tall gray-haired colonel was soft-spoken and polite. But the two soldiers of fortune knew that few Latins of any variety ever invited anyone into their private homes to discuss business if it could be avoided. Hence, it was obvious the colonel didn't want it official when he met them at his home after dark instead of at his office.

He'd sent his family off somewhere and set up his library as an ad hoc war room, with a wall map of Costa Rica thumbtacked over a wall of books. After seating them in comfortable leather chairs and serving them Scotch and Havanas, the colonel used a desk ruler for a pointer as he got right down to business, saying, ''As you may be able to see at this scale, Gentlemen, we share about a hundred and fifty miles of border, some of it disputed, with our friends to the south. Fortunately, most of it's impractical for wheeled vehicles or even cavalry. Our own limited official forces are dug in here, here, and here. We don't expect anyone to openly attack our flags or uniforms if it can be avoided.''

He moved his pointer to where the contour lines ran closer together and added, ''There's a barely passable mountain route across the border here, in the central highlands. We don't have the troops to hold it against desperate or determined invaders.''

''Is anyone covering it at all, Sir?'' asked Captain Gringo.

Vegas nodded and said, ''Yes. One company of our usual border guards. Enough to stop smugglers, perhaps. Not enough to stand up to a guerrilla army or the Colombians chasing them. If we move troops from the other border crossings to back them up, we shall of course end up with *four* tempting targets instead of one. Our own intelligence agents south of the border tell us we are not the first or only ones who've noted this gap in our border defenses. So we're expecting the trouble in the area I'd like to send you to. Has Lieutenant Verrier here explained the, ah, details to you, Captain Gringo?''

The tall American nodded but said, ''The finances sound right, Sir. But I've still got some questions.''

''Ask away, then. I have nothing to hide.''

Captain Gringo rose and moved over to the map to point with his finger before saying, ''I see other passes through those border hills, Sir. Here and here. What's to prevent someone from invading you those ways?''

Vegas smiled wearily and replied, ''Where would they go then? If you will look more closely to the north, you will see those two valleys end in uninhabited and most steep rain forest. The danger to us via the one vital passage, here, is that once they are over our border they are free to just keep going, into the coffee plantations, here, and as far north as San José itself!"

Captain Gringo nodded and said, "When you're right you're right, Sir. But, okay, what about this bridge, here, just inside your border? If I have those contour lines right, they'd have one hell of a deep canyon to cross, flying, if you simply blew that trestle!"

The colonel nodded and said, "True. But bridges cost money and lives. We spent many colónes, and lost seven or eight workers, building that bridge the *first* time. So we'd like to keep it if we can. Our own border guards of course have orders to demolish it should you not be able to stop an invasion in force. But we have hired you in hopes you won't *let* anyone get that far north, eh?"

Captain Gringo said, "Hm, that might be a selling point if we can get anyone on the other side to listen. Do I have your permission to hold parleys with anyone I can, Sir?"

The colonel looked pained and said, "As a mere guerrilla, I mean no disrespect, you are free to do anything you wish to take advantage of other irregulars. I don't see how you could parley with the Colombian army, since you have no official status with *any* army and since international law gives them the right to fire on any irregular, with or without a truce flag in his hand."

Captain Gringo shrugged and said, "Oh, well, one out of two ain't bad. Let's talk about this unofficial whatever you want us to lead, Sir. For openers, how come it has to be unofficial? Why couldn't we just put Costa Rican battle kit on everybody in the first place? Might stop the Colombians, at least, from crossing the border without a proper declaration of war."

Vegas sighed and said, "That's the way I'd do it, if it were up to me alone. Unfortunately, or perhaps fortunately for my country, Costa Rica has a strong civilian government, with a built-in distrust of any military, including its own. That's why we have so few troops of any kind, and that's why my civilian superiors hit the roof when we even dared to suggest the idea of, ah, irregular patriots."

Captain Gringo shot a thoughtful look at Gaston, who cleared his throat and asked, "May one inquire, très man to man, if your civilian superiors in point of fact know anything at *all* about this skullduggery?"

The colonel looked uncomfortable and replied, "I have official approval to for God's sake do *something*. I don't think they wish to know the fine print. In any case, it would be illegal to put Costa Rican uniforms on anyone not actually part of our military forces, and they won't allow us any more forces than we have, lest some untrustworthy officer take it into his head to change a constitution most of us are content with at the moment, eh?"

Captain Gringo sat back down and took a luxurious drag on the expensive cigar before he said, "You'd know best how to run your country, Sir. Let's talk about *defending* it. Just what do we have to work with?"

Vegas reached inside his tunic to produce some papers as he said, "We've recruited an irregular battalion for you. Enlisted men, of course, Costa Ricans who've either served a hitch in the guard before or express a willingness to learn. Coffee prices are down this year. These are the names of the soldiers of fortune we've approached to serve as your company commanders."

He handed the list to Captain Gringo, who passed it on to Gaston and asked the colonel, "What about heavy weapons, Sir?"

Vegas looked uncomfortable and replied, "One machine gun per company, chambered of course to fire the same .30-30 ammo as the men's Krag rifles."

"That's it? Oh, right, if your superiors were willing to spend real money, they could just blow the fucking bridge and save a lot of bother. So let's talk about the bother. Just how many people are we supposed to stop with a light battalion of greenhorns, Colonel?"

Vegas shrugged and answered, "We have no figures on irregulars. At least three separate guerrilla bands are being mopped up at the moment by the Colombian regulars as this season's revolution winds down. The Colombian army has at best no more than a battalion, like yours, close enough to our border to worry about.''

Captain Gringo swore softly and protested, ''Colonel, a battalion of regulars is *nothing* like ours. We're talking about real soldiers. Good ones. We've tangled with them in the past, and, I don't know how to tell you this, but Colombia uses experienced officers, leading well-trained legged-up infantrymen. Unlike your government, Colombia's current junta ain't so popular. So their army gets to fight a lot, and you know what they say about practice making perfect!''

Gaston, meanwhile, had been scanning the list of proposed officers for the Costa Rican irregulars. So he cut in, ''Merde alors, may I please be excused for the rest of the war, teacher?''

They both looked at him with raised eyebrows. So he explained, ''I know these très adorable rogues all too well. Dutch Lansford, here, is all right. We served together in Mexico, and since he's still alive, he must be doing something right. If I knew who Jack the Ripper was, I'd rather serve with him at my back than this Jacques Latrec, an escapee from Devil's Island who deserved to stay there!''

Vegas said, ''He comes highly recommended as a soldier of fortune.''

Gaston shook his head and said, ''Not by *me*, bless his sticky fingers and amusing way with women. The species of insect is an armed robber, a rapist, and an assassin for hire. But a *soldier?* Surely you jest! Not even a gang of bank robbers would want our adorable Jacques. He'd cut his mother's throat in her sleep, just for practice!''

Captain Gringo told Vegas, ''Gaston's the man to ask, when it comes to knockaround guys down here. I wouldn't trust any man Gaston doesn't trust. Sometimes I'm not too sure about Gaston.''

The little Frenchman said, ''Merci. This Canadian, Menzies, won't do, either. Whoever told you Menzies was a soldier was full of merde. He may be of some use to the Royal Mounties, if they ever catch him. There would seem to be a law up there regarding crimes of passion."

Vegas looked uncomfortable and said, "I mean no disrespect, Gentlemen, but *most* of you soldiers of fortune seem to have, ah, criminal records."

Gaston smiled pleasantly and said, "Oui, but if you are discussing my adorable child here, or me, murder is a necessary skill in our profession. But a good soldier kills in cold blood, when he *has* to. Our Menzies kills because he is très *nuts!* Homicidal maniacs no doubt have their place in the scheme of things. But not leading troops, and they say when people try to lead Menzies, he is prone to dangerous fits."

Captain Gringo said, "Okay, we've got at least one company commander and we can see how many of our Costa Ricans can pass on sensible orders. Let's get back to them. Naturally they're going to insist on dragging pussy along, Colonel?"

Vegas shrugged and said, "All Latin American military expeditions include adelitas. Having female companionship along cuts down on homosexuality, desertion, rape, and so forth, eh?"

"Yeah, and it cuts down on *efficiency* pretty good, too. But I know better than to argue. A peon soldado would just rather risk his ass by soldiering sloppy than leave his ass behind. What kind of weapons have the girls been issued, the same Krag rifles, I hope?"

Vegas looked astounded and asked, "Who ever heard of arming *adelitas*, for God's sake?"

"Me, for openers," Captain Gringo replied. "I don't lead anybody into battle unarmed. Look, Colonel, I know this may come as a shock to you, but when the enemy spots a helpless she-male on the field of battle, he can get rude as hell to her. Trust us on this. Up in Mexico, one time, armed camp followers came in handy as hell after most of our men had been picked off."

"But, Captain Gringo, women don't know how to shoot guns!"

"Anybody can learn to shoot a gun in five minutes if somebody will only show them which end the bullet comes out of, Colonel. A dame may not shoot so *good*. But it's better than not being able to shoot at all when somebody comes at you with his own gun and hard-on pointed your way!"

He took another nostalgic drag on his smoke and added, "Besides, arming the adelitas will double our fire power, and we may need a lot of that if your figures are at all accurate."

The colonel still looked mighty dubious. So Gaston said, "Eh bien, you recruited us because you hoped we were professionals who might know what we were doing. Do we do the job our way, or would you rather get someone else who shares your, ah, traditional views?"

Vegas said, "That is not the problem. Arming the camp followers as well makes sense, now that you've explained the advantages. The problem is where I'm to get the additional weapons on such short notice. I told you how little my superiors are willing to spend on this, ah, experiment."

He noted the looks that passed between his guests and added quickly, "Your own checks have of course been made out to you. You'll have plenty of time to cash them here in town before you march out."

Suiting deeds to his words, the colonel produced two certified checks from his tunic and held them out to Captain Gringo. The tall American shook his head and said, "Before we accept the front money, we look at the fine print, Colonel. When do we inspect our troops?"

"Most of them have already been assembled. Your battalion should be ready to move by, say, nine tomorrow morning? At the old parade grounds?"

Captain Gringo rose to his feet and said, "Bueno. We'll be there with bells on. If we don't see everybody there with weapons and ammo, plus at least one mountain mortar section and, oh yeah, at least a cartload of grub, the deal's off. Let's go, Gaston.''

As the small Frenchman rose, Colonel Vegas protested, ''Wait! I don't know how the devil I'm to get such extra combat gear together on such short notice! I'll have to get in touch with my civilian superiors, and if I can't convince them . . .''

''Convince 'em, Colonel,'' Captain Gringo cut in, adding, ''otherwise, you'll have to find some other suckers. Gaston and me only fight wars for money. We don't sign up to commit *suicide!*''

Colonel Vegas must have been a good talker. The next morning, Captain Gringo and Gaston legged it to the old parade grounds, left over from the Spanish colonial era, to find the colonel and some other neatly dressed Costa Rican officers presiding over what looked more like a ragged mob than a guerrilla battalion. But the soldiers of fortune noted with approval, as they surveyed the men and women hunkered in the shade of the cactus hedge around the field, that all had rifles across their laps, slung over their shoulders, just lying in the grass beside them, or whatever. Better yet, an old brass-barreled four-inch mountain mortar stared up at the sky near an overloaded two-wheel cart full of other goodies.

Captain Gringo saw no reason to dress down his bewildered troops just yet. So he let them get some more rest on their asses as he and Gaston joined the officers around the cart. He nodded respectfully to the colonel and asked, ''Are the machine guns under that tarp, Sir?'' But before the colonel could answer, one of his junior officers, a snippy-looking major, snapped, ''Don't you know enough to salute a superior officer, Yanqui!''

The pleasant Colonel Vegas looked embarrassed. Captain Gringo smiled at the puffed-up major and said, ''Gee, I bet your folks are proud of you in that uniform, Hijo.

But didn't anyone ever tell you that only guys *in* some army, *in* uniform, get to salute anybody?"

"You call me Hijo? You dare?"

"If you don't like my manners, Major, I suggest you get back to the officers' club poco tiempo. This hot morning sun seems to be getting to you. Your face is all red."

Then he turned his back on the jerk-off, aware that Gaston was covering it, and again asked the colonel about the machine guns. The colonel must have made a silent signal with his eyes as he told a more-sensible-looking lieutenant to peel the tarp. Because the next time Captain Gringo bothered to look, the red-faced major was gone.

The three machine guns were Belgian copies of the original Maxim patent, and, better yet, someone had thought to clean them and set the head spacing right for a change. The ammo-belt boxes read .30-30. Captain Gringo broke open one and tried a belt in each breech just the same. They fit. Things were looking up this morning.

Then Gaston nudged him and said, "Regardez, here comes Dutch Lansford, which sounds reasonable, with Menzies, which does not."

Captain Gringo turned to face the two linen-suited figures coming across the grass stubble toward them as he asked the colonel how come Menzies was here.

Vegas said, "We sent word to both Menzies and Latrec that you would not require their services after all. I don't understand this."

Apparently Dutch Lansford didn't, either. He looked uneasy as they got within speaking distance, trying to tell them something with his eyes as he said, "Morning, Colonel, Walker, Gaston. Heard you guys needed help with a border war."

Captain Gringo nodded and said, "You heard right. Welcome aboard." Then he smiled politely at the Canadian who'd tagged along and added, "Sorry, Menzies. We don't need you this trip."

At closer range, he could see why they wouldn't need him. Gaston's mild observation that the man was a dangerous lunatic hadn't prepared him for just how ugly and wild-eyed Menzies was in the flesh. The Canadian fugitive and self-styled soldier of fortune was about an inch shorter and six inches broader than the big but well-proportioned Captain Gringo. Menzies needed a shave and something to calm his nerves as he sneered, "So you're the famous Captain Gringo. You don't look like much from where *I* stand, Yank!"

So Captain Gringo put him on the ground with a left hook and, as Gaston reached thoughtfully inside his jacket, said, "No. We're going to settle this fist-city style. Ain't that right, Menzies?"

The big Canadian sat up, looking more astounded than hurt, and blurted, "Why, dammit, you . . . *hit* me!"

"I'm glad you noticed, Menzies. Now that I have your undivided attention, here's how the rest of it goes. If you want to just get up and walk away, that's Jake with me. If you want to put up your dukes, that's even better. I can see by the bulge under your jacket that we're both shoulder rigged. I won't kill you unless you go for your gun. I *will* if you do. So what's it going to be?"

Menzies got cautiously back to his feet, leaving his sombrero on the ground as he asked slyly, "How do I know you won't draw on me when I start kicking the shit out of you?"

"That's a fair question. Gaston, cover us both while we take off our gun rigs, will you?"

As Gaston's own .38 materialized in his small bony fist, one of the Costa Rican officers started to protest. But Vegas snapped in Spanish, "Let them have it out. I think I know what is going on. All those peon guerrillas are watching with undivided attention, too, see?"

Captain Gringo tossed his .38 double-action into the cart with the more imposing weaponry. Menzies removed his jacket and gun rig with the bullfighter flourishes of the born bully as he, too, enjoyed the audience.

He folded the jacket, bent to place it on the stubble with

his folded gun rig atop it, then straightened up part way to charge Captain Gringo, screaming like the maniac he was!

Captain Gringo met his rush with an elbow block and another sucker punch that should have decked him. But while Menzies was a lousy boxer for a guy who spent so much time hurting people, he was just too crazy to go down. Captain Gringo slammed a right cross through his wide-open windmilling and felt sure, as his knuckles caved in a cheekbone with a sickening crunch, that the fight was about over.

It wasn't. Menzies bored in, accepting a couple more knockout punches for a saner citizen, and used his superior weight to bull inside Captain Gringo's guard and grab him in a bear hug. A *big* bear's hug.

As Menzies tried to knee him, Captain Gringo twisted his hips to block, grunting, "Heavens, not on the first date!" and then, as long as he had his hip against the heavier man's center of gravity anyway, twisted further to hip toss the asshole on his ass.

"Kick him!" Gaston pleaded, as Captain Gringo stepped back from his fallen foe politely, leaving the next move up to Menzies as the big Canadian considered it from his own lower point of view. Menzies shook his head like a bull with a face full of flies, rolled over on his hands and knees, and glared up like a confused but very angry beast, his already ugly face a mass of torn flesh and dripping blood.

Gaston shouted, "Now, Dick, *now!* You'll never get a better chance to put his fucking head over the goalpost!"

But Captain Gringo told him to shut up and Menzies growled, "I'm going to kill you, Yank!" as he came up off the dusty stubble like a springing jaguar!

But now Captain Gringo had his style, or lack of it, pretty pat. So he knew enough to circle rather than to try to stop the wild charges by simply meeting them flat-footed. It was harder to throw a knockout punch, dancing Gentleman Jim style. But they added up, aiming at such a wide-open windmiller, and if he couldn't put the maniac away with one punch, he sure could make hash out of his face. So he did.

By now the peones were on their feet for a better look, and one of them must have known or guessed who was fighting whom, if not exactly why, because when Captain Gringo put Menzies on his knees in a moment with a crushing jab, someone yelled, "Viva Captain Gringo! Kick him in his cojones and piss on his mother's grave!"

This must have annoyed Menzies. He suddenly had a knife in his hand he hadn't thought to mention before. As Captain Gringo danced back thoughtfully, calling out to Gaston, "No! I'll handle it!" Menzies gargled between bloody lips, "I'll show them your cojones, you motherfucker! On the *ground!*"

Captain Gringo sighed and said, "I wanted to keep this friendly, Pal. But if that's the way you want it . . ."

Then he spun one mosquito-booted heel, and as Menzies bored in with the blade slashing wildly, Captain Gringo lashed out with the other boot heel, breaking the big Canadian's thigh bone just above the knee.

That was enough to put even a homicidal maniac on the ground for the foreseeable future. But Menzies went on roaring curses and spitting blood. So Captain Gringo stepped closer, stomped his knife hand, breaking all his fingers as well as his grip, and as he kicked away the knife he said, "I dunno, Menzies. You're just no fucking good to anybody, now."

So as everyone watched with bated breath, Captain Gringo simply kicked Menzies full in the face, flattening him full length, and then calmly placed the instep of a boot across the helpless bully's Adam's apple to crunch it like a beetle.

Menzies drummed the ground with his heels for a few seconds, then pissed his pants and just lay limp as Captain Gringo calmly walked over to the cart to get back his gun. One of the Costa Rican officers made the sign of the cross and murmured, "Madre de Dios, is he . . . ?" and Colonel

Vegas told him not to ask stupid questions in front of visitors.

Putting away his .38, Captain Gringo asked the colonel if anyone expected him to explain what had just happened to anyone official. The tall gray-haired Costa Rican smiled wanly and said, "I'll take care of the paperwork here. Frankly, I'll feel safer after all of you have left civilization for the front."

Captain Gringo nodded, turned away, and called out to the now most nervous-looking guerrillas all around, "Bueno, battalion, atención! Fall in and cover down! Hombres in company formations; adelitas back against the hedgerow and shut up until I get around to inspecting cunt! What are you espantajos idiotas waiting for? *Move* it, damn your lazy nalgas!"

They moved it, laughing and cursing like good-natured pirates, as Captain Gringo and Gaston took up the usual parade-ground posts of commander and adjutant. Dutch Lansford came unstuck and dogtrotted over to get in front of one of the milling bunches that might turn into companies, once they had the outfit pounded into shape. Behind them, one of the Costa Rican officers murmured to Colonel Vegas, "My God, they told us he was a ruffian. But that big Yanqui's *really* rough! Why did he have to kill that pobrecito just now? I saw no real need to, once he was down."

Colonel Vegas said, calmly, "That is why *he* is leading this band of cutthroats instead of you, Lieutenant. I doubt, now, he'll have to fight anyone *else* in the battalion, eh?"

Captain Gringo marched his new command south out of San José by the considerable light of the noonday sun, and if anyone felt less than enthusiastic about missing his or her siesta, tough shit. Any number of people could be spreading half-ass gossip about their so-called secret mission by now, of course. But the empty streets and shuttered windows they saw all around as they got the show on the road might serve to keep the gossip half-ass, at least.

Having spent half the morning shaping the column up, Captain Gringo had them moving in good order. Lansford had command of the heavy-weapons detail and A Company. B and C had been placed under the astounded commands of a former Costa Rican guard corporal called Moncada and Ex-Lance Corporal Frutos. They'd been told to select their own company-platoon and squad leaders, since they probably knew the others best, right now.

The adelitas of course brought up the rear, getting to carry most of the gear of their soldados. Captain Gringo could only hope no spy determined enough to skip siesta was about, lest it be noted that each skirted dependent attached informally to his informal command had been issued a spanking-new Krag rifle and crossed ammo bandoleras. He wanted it to be a surprise if and when someone found out the hard way that his guerrilla battalion had twice the fire power one might expect.

Lansford, who hadn't been there the time Captain Gringo and Gaston had stood off Mexican federales with hastily armed and instructed women, was still dubious. But he had enough to worry about without pestering the women to the rear. The Costa Rican military hadn't seen fit to issue them mules for the mountain mortar and supply cart and the peones pulling them down the dusty road under the searing tropic sun were bitching and balking worse than mules. Lansford was saved from having to shoot a whiner who simply let go of a cart shaft and threw himself into the shaded ditch, explaining that he had a heart condition, when Captain Gringo, at the head of the column, raised a hand to halt it and called back, "Bueno. We're well out of town and there's no sense being *silly* about this. Commanders, move your people off the road and dismiss them for a trail break. You there, in the ditch. Get off your ass and help get that cart and the mortar under cover. I'm not going to say it twice."

Then, not looking back to see if his commands were

being obeyed to the letter, he moved off the road into the shade and sat down cross-legged under a gum tree to light a smoke. Gaston or Dutch would tell him if anyone really fucked up. He knew it was too early to expect them to toe the mark or let them think they were getting away with anything. He hoped he wouldn't have to set any further examples. His knuckles still hurt. But he knew he probably would. There was always at least one natural troublemaker in every squad, and a battalion added up to a mess of squads. He'd just gotten his claro smoking right when he spotted some kind of trouble headed his way through the trees and got wearily back to his feet.

Two of his armed adelitas were frog-marching a third, unarmed girl in an expensive and impractical blue dress between them. Giving even a woman a gun seemed to make her want to play soldier. So the biggest of the three shot him a really silly salute and announced, "We found this puta skulking about the edge of camp, Captain Gringo. We thought you might wish for to interview her before we shot her, no?"

The tall Yank repressed an outright laugh as he viewed the frightened captive and said, "Bueno. I'll take charge of the prisoner. You two report back to your posts."

"Our *what*, Captain Gringo?"

"Go sit under a tree or something. We're not going to stay here long. So try and rest your shapely shapes. I don't think this muchacha can lick me, do you?"

The older, tougher adelitas laughed and moved off through the trees as he told the now-terrified girl to sit down for God's sake and did so himself. She hesitated, then sank to her knees in the nearby grass, as he stared at her impassively.

It didn't hurt. She was a pretty little thing with more white than Indian blood in her. She had the slimmer waist and bigger breasts of a white woman, too. She was trying not to cry as she stammered, "For why would you wish to shoot me, Captain Gringo? I have done nothing bad."

"You know what I am called, Señorita?"

"Sí, you are the famous Captain Gringo and you are marching south for to fight bad hombres. I wished for to join your army, not to do anything wicked to you and your people!"

He *let* himself laugh now and asked, "What else do you want to be when you grow up, a fireman? How old are you, Chiquita, sixteen?"

"I shall *soon* be sixteen." She pouted, adding, "I know you have younger people than me marching with you, Captain Gringo!"

He sighed and said, "Yeah, they recruited this bunch in a hurry. But, no offense, Gatita, you're a little more, ah, sheltered-looking than my other ragged orphans. What did you do, run away from home?"

She nodded sadly and said, "Sí, I had to. My padre is not a bad man, but he kept beating me and beating me and . . ."

"Come on," he cut in, "you don't look like a maltreated child. You look like a wayward girl from a good home who's had a fuss with her parents and . . ."

Then she shut him up good, by unbuttoning her bodice and giving him just a peek at her firm but ample young breasts before turning her naked back to him, protesting, "Does this look to you as if I am a liar, Captain Gringo!"

He whistled softly as he stared at the vivid whip marks across her otherwise creamy skin and answered soberly, "Button up, dammit. I'm convinced. What on earth did you do to rate a licking like that, Gatita?"

She sobbed, "*Nada!* I did nothing at all! But my father would not listen to me. He kept beating me and beating me for to make me confess. But I had *done* nothing, so how could I confess?"

"He sure must have wanted you to. What was it your father accused you of?"

"Quién sabe? He never told me. He seemed to think I should *know* what I had done, and every time I told him I did not, he hit me again! My mother finally saved me, by telling me to go with God while he went for to get a bigger whip from the stable. Alas, *she* thinks I am wicked, too. But she did not wish for to see me beaten to death and . . .''

"Hold it," Captain Gringo cut in, as a horrible thought crossed his mind. He asked, "How are you called, Señorita?" and when she said her name was *Maria Castro* he swore softly to himself and added, "Yeah, you would look like someone else I've met, at a distance, in a red dress."

"You know about my fiesta dress? You have seen me before, Captain Gringo?"

"Not exactly, but close enough. Oh boy, what do we do now?"

"You will let me march with you as an adelita now?"

He frowned and said, "That sounds almost as bad. Do you know just what an adelita is, Maria?"

"Sí, I have heard the most romantico songs about faithful adelitas and their brave soldados. It sounds like much more fun than being beaten to death by my poor crazy padre, no?"

"I'm still working on that," he replied, adding, "I don't see how the hell I can send you home alone. And I can't go with you to explain."

"What could you explain to my poor crazy padre, Captain Gringo?"

"Forget it. He probably wouldn't listen, and I'd hate to hurt him more. But look, Maria, a camp follower isn't exactly what one may have gathered from old war ballads. I don't know how to phrase it more delicately. So, all right, do you know what a puta is?"

She blushed beet red and lowered her eyes as she stammered, "Oh. For why is there nothing like *that* in the old army songs, por favor?"

"Most songs are intended for mixed company. Laying out all the cards, face up, an adelita is a camp follower who might or might not be married to the soldado she carries and cooks for, and keeps company in camp at night with. There'd be no point in having a woman along who wasn't willing to perform all the duties, repeat *all* the duties, of a, frankly, sort of stupid slut. I guess you'd have to be raised down here to see just what the hell adelitas *get* out of following armies around. But that's what they do. I hope I haven't shocked you, Señorita.''

She sighed and said, ''You have. Very much. But what am I to do? I can never go home again, can I?''

''I don't see how you can, either, damn my horny hide. All right, I owe you. So here's what we'll have to do. . . .''

''You *owe* me, Señor?'' she cut in, her big brown eyes staring up at him bemused and trusting, as he shut her up and added, ''Just take my word for it, Maria. Here's what we'd better do. I'm recruiting you as my own adelita. That would usually make you boss adelita, but don't press your luck with the others. Most of them could snatch you bald headed before you knew what was happening. Just stick close to me for now and let me do the talking, got it?''

''Sí, I think so. But if I am to be your adelita, does that mean I have to be, ah, *sinful* with you? Forgive me, I mean no disrespect, but you are very big and tough-looking and . . . I am sorry, I am frightened. I want my mamacita!''

He took her in his arms to comfort her, patting her shoulder as he soothed, ''Don't cry, dammit. Nobody's going to make you do anything you don't want to. It's a private joke, see? We'll just tell everyone I've claimed you. Nobody else will bother you. Then, as soon as I figure out where in hell you'll be safe . . .''

Then he looked up sheepishly, as Gaston's sardonic voice cut in, ''Merde alors, how do you *do* it, Dick? Do you pop them out of your hat like rabbits or do they simply follow you around all the time?''

Captain Gringo said, ''Gaston, this is Maria. Remember that scene under our window last night?''

''Ah, at last I see the light. Which one is she?''

Captain Gringo switched to English to say, ''Ixnay. Innocent bystander.'' Then, more politely, he added in Spanish, ''She's coming with us as my adelita. Pass the word.''

"Eh bien, but you should be ashamed of yourself," Gaston said in English.

In the same language, Captain Gringo said, "Don't worry. I am."

They hit the trail again and marched on south, for days and nights. The days went pretty well. Most of his people were already used to hard labor and legged up quickly. The desertion rate was surprisingly low for irregulars. During trail breaks Captain Gringo instructed a squad from each company on the care and feeding of the Maxim machine gun. A standard machine-gun squad consisted of two men to man the weapon, two more to step in should either gunner get hit, with the others trained to help dig in the nest and then cover it with their rifles out on either flank.

Since one never knew when the enemy would get lucky, he made sure every man in a squad could fill in as machine gunner or loader should the need arise. Having neither the ammo to spare nor a safe firing range to work with, he had to teach them dry-fire. But if they ranged the weapons right and fired sensible bursts with the traverse and elevation knobs locked, one could at least hope.

Gaston worked on whipping his gun crew into shape, cursing them and the antique mountain mortar in Spanish, French, Arabic, and, if need be, Yiddish. The kids he picked caught on pretty fast, once they got over their mortal fear of the sometimes excitable little Frenchman. There was nothing Gaston could do to improve the gun and its dubious ammo. The mortar was left over from the American Civil War or the American Revolution, according to whether one accepted the ordnance dates on its breech or Gaston's word that they were an obvious forgery. Whatever it was, the mortar was set in a heavy block of pickled oak one removed from the carriage and placed flat against the ground when it was time to fire. The tube could not be depressed less than forty-five degrees, which was what made it a mortar. The gunner was supposed to range by dropping more or less fist-sized silk-encased powder charges down the tube before ramming home the shrapnel or penetrating HE shell, depending on whom one wanted to disturb most. They'd been issued both, as well as some common rounds, or solid slugs Gaston had disposed of in a ditch as "merde" the first day to lighten their baggage. Both kinds of exploding shells were fused the same way, albeit timed so that the shrapnel shells burst above and the others below ground level, hopefully. It depended on how old the primitive fuses were. They were simply plugs of softwood impregnated with quick-match nitrate. When one of his students asked Gaston why the fuse plugs were set in the noses instead of the bases of the shells, Gaston accused him of habitually infecting small children with the clap, before explaining, "If the fuses were screwed into the bases of the shells, the propelling charge would très obviously drive them up into the shell and you would have a most unamusing premature ignition, as anyone but an imbecile with his head up his own derriere should be able to see! The plug in the nose cone is, of course, ignited when the whole tube is filled with flame during the shell's short stay there. You will regard there are neither rifle lands nor driving bands to seal this antique's. Forget how the no-doubt useless shells are supposed to explode. You there, Fidelito, tell us all how one fires this stupid species of *gun!*"

"With another fuse, through that little hole you showed us, Señor?"

"Sacrebleu! Must I spend the rest of my few remaining years among the deaf? A mortar is supposed to be a rapidfire weapon, you slow-learning son of not only a camel but an *ugly* one! You do not *fuse* the touch hole. You jam your gunner's pick down it to puncture the silk of the bottom charge. Then you inject loose powder from your gunner's horn to fill the touch hole, touch the hole with the tip of your cigar, and, voilà, if the breech doesn't blow up in your face and kill you, the shell may soar très dramatique to kill somebody else. Are there any other questions, my adorable retarded children?"

"Sí; for why are those powder charges encased in silk, Señor? Is not silk most expensive?"

"Oui, *war* is expensive. Silk is the only wrapping material we have that burns completely in a discreet poof, leaving no smoldering sparks in the tube between firings. Do I really have to tell any of you what would happen if you dropped fresh charges down on smoldering rags?"

He didn't, and was secretly pleased that his illiterate but willing pupils were asking questions. Soldiers who thought they already knew all the answers got killed a lot, and tended to take others with them, on their own side.

Dutch Lansford, whose military skills were mostly infantry, drilled the men and women during trail breaks, separately, after trying it coed once and noting how much giggling and grab-assing could foul up monkey drill.

Dutch was an erstwhile U.S. Seventh Infantry sergeant major who'd retired early, over a stockade fence, after breaking the jaw of a chicken-shit shavetail who'd been harassing the troops above and beyond the call of duty or sanity. Since then he'd served in a dozen armies, including the German African colonial, hence the nickname, so he knew how to whip total greenhorns into shape without killing them and was, like Gaston, secretly pleased with his current raw material.

Though dubious of the idea at first, Lansford was fair-minded enough to admit that some of the tough little adelitas seemed natural-born infantrymen, once you allowed for more-delicate stature and the way they handled a piss call. The girls, in turn, were delighted to be taken so seriously by a man, a gringo officer at that, who didn't want to lay them. Or at least not *all* of them. They agreed it was only fair that Fulgencia and fat Mirta sleep with Captain Lansford once their original soldados had deserted.

Weaklings who dropped out of a marching column did so mostly because they were tired of carrying so much shit. So they'd left behind extra gear as well as extra pussy, and the new female recruit, Maria Castro, looked more military now with her own bandoleras crossed on her considerable chest and a bayoneted bolt-action Krag almost as tall as she was on her shoulder. Unlike most of the other adelitas, Maria was hopeless as a soldier, male or female. But Dutch figured he'd better go easy on her, since she was Captain Gringo's new adelita.

That part was what made the nights less pleasant than the days for Captain Gringo. It was hell to share a lean-to and bedroll with a homesick virgin. For that's what she was, no matter what that nasty little bitch had said about her under a mimosa tree. He'd found out the first night. There were dames who put on an act and there were dames who cried real tears.

He knew, as a man of the world, that he could have her if he really worked on her, taking advantage of her innocence. The poor dumb kid would buy anything her now only protector told her, from, "Can't you see we're married in the eyes of God?" to the cruder, "If you really loved me you'd be willing to prove it by letting me knock you up."

But, dammit, she *trusted* him, with doglike devotion that increased every mile of the march, and he probably *would* knock her up, since she was as ignorant about sex as she was about everything else from bayonet drill to building a campfire with dry wood for chrissake. So he got to sleep on his belly a lot, with her soft little body snuggled against his, trustingly, and his body trying to bore a hole through the ground cloth.

Worse yet, everyone else in the column thought he was getting laid every night. Since Maria was pretty as a picture as well as too dumb to be running around without a leash, the men shot envious glances at them, and the women, naturally, shot lewd comments and flirtatious glances he couldn't take them up on. And a couple of the recently deserted adelitas weren't bad.

Why they were still tagging along was a mystery as well as a growing problem to Captain Gringo. Gaston, who'd solved part of the problem by adopting a good cook and a reputedly great lay who'd lived up to her disgraceful reputation, suggested they let the matter take care of itself for now, pointing out, "The poor little tramps have no place else to go, in a pinch can fire a rifle, and who can say, this early, who may yet desert or die, male or female?"

They were discussing the matter alone, seated on a fallen log four days out of San José and about forty feet from the nearest campfire. So Captain Gringo didn't have to whisper as he exhaled a drag of smoke and said, "I was thinking about sending Maria back with a couple of the dames we don't really need. By now her old man may have cooled down, right?"

Gaston shook his head and said, "Wrong. Trust me on the Latin sense of honor, Dick. I assure you I have no honor at all, myself, but I know the très fatigué species her fat father is. If he beat her half to death even *before* she ran away, he'll no doubt do a better job if he ever gets his hands on her again, non?"

Captain Gringo took a weary drag on his claro and let it out before he nodded and said, "That's what *she* thinks, too. But what the fuck am I supposed to do with a fourteen-year-old virgin, dammit?"

"Merde alors, what a stupid question to ask of a dirty old man! But how did she get to be fourteen? Did she not say she was *sixteen,* when she joined us a few days ago?"

"She lied. Since she's found out I don't bite, she's started to level with me more, damn her cute little ass. I'll shit you not, by now I'd give serious consideration to deflowering a *sixteen*-year-old *nun!* But even a guy with a hard-on has to draw the line *some* damned where, and, aside from being too young, she's too sweetly stupid. Nobody but a rotten bastard would take advantage of the poor little thing."

Gaston blew a thoughtful smoke ring and observed, "This cruel world is filled with rotten bastards, Dick. Sooner or later she's going to run into one, and why should he have all the fun?"

Captain Gringo grimaced and said, "I was telling my-self that just the other night, or maybe my twitching pecker was telling me I was just being an idiot who liked to suffer beyond common sense. It was a pretty good rationalization, and she was pretty tempting, laying there beside me helpless as a kitten. If this shit keeps up much longer, I'm probably going to be a shit. I'm only a saint, after all, not a martyr. So tell me how the hell we get rid of her, Gaston. I'm stuck."

Gaston shrugged and said, "Assuming you don't wish to simply shoot her, one supposes we could drop her off at the next town we come to. There are several on the map to choose from before we get into the really wild country near the border. You know, of course, what happens then to a strange young femme without local family connec-tions. But with luck, the pimp who picks her up won't be too hard on her. She's très attractive. She may even find a male protector who'll wish to keep her all to himself, hein?"

"Boy, you paint a pretty picture, Gaston."

"Oui, it's a very pretty world out there. An Hispanic girl without a chaperon, *both* under the protection of a reasonably macho *male*, is ipso facto a whore, to be treated as such by one and all."

"Swell. That leaves marriage or a nunnery. I sure as shit ain't about to marry her. Maybe there's a convent we could drop her off at between here and the border?"

"Mais non, and if there was, she'd be just as happy being beaten by her father. The Spanish Church is très severe on runaway girls, since, to be fair, few nice Hispanic girls run away in the first place. The mother superior, if she took Maria in at all, would be duty bound to contact her family to inquire if they wished her back or simply burned at the stake on the spot."

"Oh, come on, Gaston. They don't do *that* anymore!"

"Well, perhaps they'd simply let her work off her penance à la Cinderella until her father came for her."

"Okay, you've convinced me, you son of a bitch."

Gaston looked hurt and said, "Temper, temper, my hard-up youth. Why does the problem have to be solved this very instant? We're still nowhere near the battle zone, and the girl seems to have no trouble keeping up with the column, hein?"

"We can't take her with us that far. She's just a kid who's led a very sheltered life, and if I even got her hurt . . ."

"Without ever having *had* her?" Gaston cut in with a sardonic smile, adding, "Face it, you fortunate devil. Go back to your lean-to and shove your tormented tool where it will make you both very happy. You know you're going to, sooner or later, if we keep her with us. You know if we ditch her along the line of march some other no-doubt vicious but more-sensible hombre is going to get it anyway, and . . ."

Captain Gringo didn't want to hit an old pal. So he got up and walked away, cursing savagely under his breath. He wasn't sure where he was going. Sooner or later he'd have to rejoin Maria if he meant to get any sleep at all tonight. It was the other sooner or later he was worried about. Jerking off in the woods wasn't the answer. It felt silly as hell and hadn't worked the night before, dammit.

As he muttered his way between the trees they'd camped among that night, a sultry voice called out softly, "Halt, who goes there!" So, when he got back inside the skin he'd nearly jumped out of, Captain Gringo identified himself and moved closer for a better look at the female picket some asshole had posted out here in the woods.

He recognized her by the faint moonlight as the adelita they called Azucar. It wasn't a real name. It meant "Sugar." It fit. Despite Indian eyes and cheekbones, Azucar's soft skin was so unusually pale, even for a blanca, that she seemed made out of marshmallow. She was resting her rifle on its butt plate by her pale bare feet, but wasn't wearing bandoleras across her chest or, come to think of it, much else. The man's shirt she wore was a couple of sizes too small for her and her big white boobs were threatening to burst the last button any minute. He tried to ignore the tingle endangering his own buttons as he stared down at her in the moonlight and tried to come up with something sensible for a commanding officer to say to a private who was giving him a hard-on.

Azucar smiled up at him and said, "I just came on duty. I am not due to be relieved for two hours, Captain Gringo. Is it true a soldado is free to make himself comfortable any way he likes while on guard, as long as he keeps his eyes peeled for the enemy?"

He laughed and said, "I doubt you should be called a *he,* for God's sake, and I'd be surprised to see any enemies this far north of the border. But I suppose Captain Lansford thinks it's good practice."

Her voice was openly lewd as she replied, "Sí, that is what he said. He said if we did not stay most alert he might catch us gilding the brick, whatever that means, if and when he makes his rounds as officer of the day." She giggled and added, "I do not think he shall be by this post tonight. He just went to bed with two women."

"Well, rank has its privileges, and you're not supposed to gossip about your officers, Azucar."

Her eyes were mocking as she said, "I know. But sometimes it is hard to resist. Forgive me, I mean no disrespect, but since my soldado deserted, two nights ago, dirty thoughts keep creeping up on me. I am, alas, a woman of some passion."

It would have taken a very stupid man some effort to miss the open invitation in both her words and her big almond eyes, and Captain Gringo wasn't stupid. But the situation was a little sticky and getting more so as he tried to decide whether to just keep walking or, please, God, work something out that wouldn't result in a howling cat fight.

He didn't want her telling the other adelitas he was a sissy or, even worse, dumb. So he leaned closer with a palm braced against the tree trunk above her soft shoulder as he said with easy familiarity he didn't feel, "I understand your problem and I'd like to help you out, as one old army buddy to another. You know you are most bonita, but . . .''

"Sí." She sighed. "Your little Maria is most bonita, too, and, naturally, most jealous?"

"Naturally, and, worse yet, I'm stuck with her. Her father is a high-ranking officer. I think she was sent along to make sure I behaved."

"Ah, that explains her elegant manners. We've been wondering about that. We all knew she was not a regular camp follower."

"Don't tell the other adelitas," he warned, knowing she would. Once he told Maria what to say, now, the other, tougher girls would treat her with more caution and he wouldn't have to watch out for her *all* the time.

As they chatted about his domestic problems, both trying to keep it casual, but both all too aware of the other's breath caressing their numb lips in the moonlight, Azucar said, "I would not wish for to get you in trouble with your official adelita. But, ah, is she all the woman a man of your size can, ah, cope with?"

He smiled, leaned even closer, and said, "Most of the time. She's a woman of considerable passion, too. Unfortunately, tonight she turned in early, with a headache or something."

"Ah, el período, eh? It is not fair, the way nature abuses us poor mujeres. Perhaps, however, that is why some men, they say, prefer to have another mujer on the side?"

He didn't answer. She reached down casually and began to toy with his belt buckle as she asked, "Would *you* wish for to have a mujer on the side, Captain Gringo?"

"Well, since you put it that way, but we'd have to be very very, ah, discreet. I wouldn't want to hurt either of your feelings, see?"

She opened his fly, took the matter firmly in hand, and sighed. "Oh, please stop teasing me, por favor!"

So he did. Her rifle fell sideways to the forest duff as her skirts rose, his pants dropped, and he tried to shove her through the tree she was braced against as he exploded inside her almost at once. She came with him, being just as hard up to begin with, and less inhibited about displaying her natural appetites. But as they came up for air, Azucar laughed in an earthy way he was getting to like better by the minute and said, "Madre de Dios, you might have warned me! Don't you think this would work better lying down, with these ridiculous garments out of the way?"

He sure did. So he took Azucar and her rifle deeper into the woods, where they found a moonlit patch of sweet-scented fern moss to do it right, and did they *ever!*

The pretty adelita figured to be fat in a few years at the rate she was going. But tonight her pale nude body formed a lush, Junoesque love wallow for a growing boy who hadn't been getting any lately. She seemed to like the way his big muscular body pinned hers to the cushion of fern moss, too, judging from the way she moved her ample, seemingly boneless hips with her pillow-soft but crushingly strong peon legs around his waist. As she started to climax again she drummed her bare heels on his bounding buttocks, pleading, "More, *more!* Oh, God, how I need for to have my pussy filled by a real man! Do you like my pussy, Señor?"

"You can call me Dick, in private, Private, and I like your pussy an awful lot. So just keep moving it like that and . . ."

"It is *your* pussy, Deek!" she cut in, rolling her head from side to side in the fern moss as he took her up on her kind gift by ejaculating in it, hard, and then, to be polite, kept going.

She moaned, "Oh, qué delicioso! If it was any longer it would kill me. If it was any shorter *I* would kill *you!* We are made perfecto for one another, so obviously when God in His wisdom made the world it was His divine plan from the beginning that you and I should fuck, no?"

He kissed her to shut her up before she said something silly. She kissed better lying down than against a tree, too. He knew she had teeth, pretty ones, since he'd seen her smile with them. But, like her bones, which had to be in there somewhere, Azucar somehow managed to make her mouth feel like a velvety vagina as she sucked his tongue farther down her soft throat than it really wanted to go. It must have given her an added thrill, too. Because just as he was starting to worry about her swallowing him alive, both ways, Azucar's mouth opened in a silent scream of ecstasy, her pale thighs gaped wide at the moon, and her vaginal muscles gripped even tighter as she groaned, "Por favor, God, when it is time for me to die, let me die like *this!*"

Then she went limp, her insides still pulsing sensuously on his shaft, and asked sweetly, "Is Maria as good a lay as me, Deek?"

He said, "Don't talk dirty. Everybody's better than everybody else when you're laying them."

She laughed lewdly and said, "Es verdad. Isn't that nice? I meant no disrespect to our head adelita, Deek. I assure you I won't even tell the others. I am a woman of passion, not a show-off."

He assumed she meant it. On the other hand, why had they nicknamed her Sugar if nobody else had had a chance to find out just how sweet she could be? There was no nice way to ask a lady how many other guys in the outfit she was being sweet to, so he didn't try.

They were just getting their breathing right again when a distant voice called out, "Hey, Post Numero Ocho! Where the hell *are* you, muchacha?" and Azucar flinched in his arms and whispered, "Oh my God! Captain Lansford *is* touring the posts tonight! Does this mean I'll be shot?"

Captain Gringo laughed and said, "Yeah, I think I can come at least one more time." Then he raised his voice to call out, "It's all right, Dutch. She's with me. I'm teaching her how to thrust with her bayonet. Carry on, Captain."

Lansford called back, "I'm sure she could use the drill, Dick. Consider me gone."

As his footsteps faded away, Azucar giggled and said,

"It must be nice to be an officer. I've never been an officer's adelita before." Then, as she felt him stop breathing against her soft chest, she quickly added, "Forgive me. I should not have said that. Are we ever to make love again, after your real adelita is well, Deek?"

He kissed her gently and said, "You're forgiven, and we're not through making love yet, if I can only get this fool thing up again. Having officers of the day yelling in my ear always confuses me for a minute."

She reached down between them and sighed as she said, "Oh, it does feel confused." Then she began to fondle his semi-erection in a manner that hinted at considerable experience in nursing the injured. He lay back sensuously on the sweet-scented ground cover and let her play with him as he went on, "About my official adelita: now that we have some ground rules out of the way, I told you how things have to be. But you're sure right about us fitting nicely together. So, if you're very good at keeping your pretty mouth shut, we might be able to work something like this out, oh, say every other night or so?"

She didn't answer. Her pretty mouth was filled at the moment. And she gave fantastic face, too, bless her sweet ass!

But he had to think about her sweet ass indeed when Azucar forced a plump knee across his chest to present her wide open groin for his full approval in the moonlight.

He approved of the view indeed. Like most men, most women, no matter how yummy, had sort of dumb-looking genitals. But Azucar was blessed with one of those rare, delightful groins that was actually *pretty*, and it was pretty obvious what she wanted him to do about it as she moved it closer to his face.

He didn't want to. She seemed like a swell kid, and Captain Gringo could be a sport with a lady he was awfully fond of. But he had no idea when the tough little adelita had last washed that love box, after *whom*, so he hoped she'd be content with friendly fingers as she treated him friendly as hell with her bobbing head and seemingly toothless oral opening down there.

He got his elbows up and hooked outside her wide-braced thighs to caress her bare buttocks with both hands teasingly before opening her vaginal lips from both sides to expose her moist inner opening and wet turgid clit, quivering in anticipation. The he began to strum her old banjo with one hand as he moved first two, then three, then four fingers in to get milked by her hot contractions. She seemed to like it. A lot. She stopped what she was doing just long enough to gasp and say, "My asshole, too, por favor!"

That sounded fair. His thumb had to go some damned place. So his one hand wound up gripping her sort of like a bowling ball as he teased her clit until they both exploded in each other's face.

Naturally, she said he was a very naughty boy to treat her poor innocent anal opening that way, once they'd calmed down again enough to share a smoke side by side again. He didn't argue. The fern moss all around was great to wipe one's hands clean on.

She handed him back the cigar and snuggled closer as she asked, "Do you do bad things to Maria's back door, too, you horrid man?"

He said, "I never discuss one lady's asshole with another. I told you not to talk dirty, Azucar."

"I'm just curious. It is natural for a woman to be curious, no?"

"That's for damned sure."

"Have you ever done it all the way like that with . . . any woman?"

"If I'm asked. It's not really a big deal or even much of a change."

"That is easy for a *man* to say. It must feel much different to the *woman,* no?"

"How the hell would I know? There's just no way a man could compare the two feelings, even if he wanted to, and I've never wanted to."

"I think *I* want to," she said, acting shy, but not too convincingly, as she added, "They say a man has not truly possessed a woman until he has come in her all three ways."

"I'm not complaining. Two out of three ain't bad, Querida."

That was a mistake, or perhaps a break. She reached down to fondle him as she murmured huskily, "Sí, I wish for to be your total querida, even if it must be a secret. I have given you my pussy, I have given you my mouth. Won't you please accept all I have left to offer, Deek?"

He laughed and said, "Well, since you put it that way..." and she laughed and rolled over on her hands and knees to let him put it that way.

In truth, it didn't work out so great, for him, at least. He was already semisated, her rectum was tight as hell, and he thought he'd never get it in that way. Then, once he did, it didn't feel any better than her sweet frontal opening. Anal sex, dog style, was better as a crime of passion than as a last hoorah for a guy whose legs were getting tired. But she seemed to enjoy it, and after they'd come that way, too, there was always the moist fern moss to wipe off with.

By the time he got back to his lean-to, Captain Gringo's legs felt sort of rubbery for some reason. He crept in quietly, so as not to disturb Maria, but the innocent teen-ager wasn't asleep and apparently hadn't been thinking innocent thoughts. As he took off all but his pants and slipped under the covers with her, he noticed that Maria was stark naked.

He said, "I wish you'd at least put your underwear on, Maria. I told you before, a man in bed with a pretty girl is only human."

She sighed and said, "Sí, I have been thinking about that. I know what a bother to you I have been up to now, Deek. I have been listening to the other adelitas. Did you know women talk dirty when men are not around?"

"I've long suspected as much. Has anyone been teasing you, Gatita?"

"No. I have been telling them, as you told me to, that we make love every night. When I told a girl called Azucar that you called me Gatita, she laughed and said *she* had a little pussy, too. What do you suppose she meant by that, Deek?"

"It's probably an inside joke. Can we go to sleep now? It's been a hard day, with more of the same ahead of us."

She started to cry.

He said, "Oh, for God's sake, what's wrong now?"

"I miss my mamacita so. I could talk to her about this mysterious business between men and women. As it is, I am so confused. I thought I knew what men and women did in bed together. But sometimes when I am pretending for to be your real adelita I must say something wrong. For the others give me such curious looks."

He pulled her closer, automatically, to comfort her as he had in the past. But up until tonight she'd been wearing clothes, for God's sake, and a soft naked female body against him had an unsettling effect, despite where he'd just been, all three ways.

Maria buried her face against his naked chest, wrapped her naked arms around him, and then, as if to twist the knife, threw a naked little thigh over his hip with her better naked features rubbing against him as she said, "Perhaps, if we did it, just a little, I would know how to pretend better, no?"

He growled, "Lord, give me strength!" and added, "Querida, there's no *little* way to have sex with a man. And once you have, you don't have to pretend he's your lover. He *is*. Am I going to fast for you, Chica?"

She sighed and said, "No. That is what I have been debating with myself and the saints all evening. I have no other choice but to be an adelita now. And an adelita has no other choice but to be a wicked woman. So, if you promise to be very very gentle and forgive me if I do not do it right..."

He cut in, "Platoon halt! About-face! You don't know what you're *talking* about, Maria!"

"I know. That is why I wish to be, how you call it, fucked? So I can talk to the other adelitas without them laughing at me. What am I supposed to do when you fuck me, Deek?"

He said, "Nothing. I'm not going to."

"Do you find me ugly, then? The others say all men wish for to fuck all the pretty mujeres they meet."

"There are *some* rules, dammit. Mothers and little sisters are off limits no matter how pretty they are. So don't *cry,* dammit! It's nothing personal. I just have to look at myself in the mirror when I shave."

She snuggled closer, her little pink nipples aroused against his naked chest now, as her young body did its level best to betray them both without her really knowing what was going on. He offered a prayer of silent thanks to an old army buddy who'd had bigger tits in the recent past. Because he knew, had he been able to get it up again at such short notice, he'd be hurting enough to have no conscience at all right now. As it was, he was sort of disappointed in his fool pecker for just *lying* there at a time like this.

He said, "Listen, Maria, you're just not cut out for army life. But there might be a way out of this fix you're in. The map says we'll be in a town called San Mateo before we hit the forget-it hills between there and the border. Do you know anyone in San Mateo?"

She shook her head against his chest and said, "I do not think so. Wait, I may have cousins on my mamacita's side in San Mateo, now that I think about it. I do not know if they are still there. My mother's sister married this man from the south and died, but before she died they had two children and I think he took them home to his people in, sí, it *might* have been San Mateo."

That sounded better than no hope at all. So he patted her bare shoulder and said, "Bueno. Now turn over and try to get some sleep. We'll talk about it in the morning."

"Can we talk about fucking in the morning, too, Deek?"

He said they could. So she kissed him like the child she still was and turned on her tummy to drop off as he turned the other way and closed his eyes. Then he thought of something and sat up to get dressed again. For there was no way in the world a grown man was about to wake up with a rested body and a morning hard-on, and *behave* himself with a pretty child who kept asking him if he wanted to fuck her!

Marching through San Mateo instead of just past it called for a slight detour to the east. But the few extra miles could be made up by cutting a few trail breaks a few minutes short, and Captain Gringo had to do *something* about Maria Castro, other than what she'd suggested.

They weren't expecting trouble yet, this far north of the border. But it was better to play safe than be sorry. So Captain Gringo gave his people a well-deserved rest in the shade of a trail-side coffee plantation and sent Dutch Lansford and a heavy patrol ahead to scout the village. He didn't expect them to report anything more ominous than an unfriendly village. So he told the adelitas not to build cooking fires and warned everyone to keep their pants on, skirts down, and heads up, and they'd be moving on poco tiempo.

Hence, he was sort of surprised and mildly worried when it seemed to take the patrol forever to report back. He'd just started worrying in earnest when they did. Dutch sat down on the fallen log beside him, lit his own cigar, and said, "We're going to have to go around, Dick."

"The villagers are unusually paranoid about their daughters and chickens?"

"Not exactly. They're under siege. Big band of ladrónes. We made it at least five hundred ragged-ass desperados dug in around the village and popping off at anything that moves in town. It gets worse. The gang has at least one automatic weapon. Heard it rattle on the far side when some villager must have moved too close to a window.''

Captain Gringo reached into his jacket, took out his ordnance map, and handed it to Dutch along with a pencil stub, saying, ''Draw me some pictures.''

Lansford said, ''Hell, Dick, it's too big a boo and for what? They're paying us to defend the border, not round up their home-grown bandits. The villagers seem to be holding out all right. San Mateo's one of those old colonial mission towns with a 'dobe wall around it, and the gang has no siege train. They're holding the corn milpas around the settlement with a ragged dug-in skirmish line. So it's a Mexican standoff for them and a good way to get smoked up by at least one machine gun for us, and for what?''

''You've forgotten which end of a pencil you use? Obviously the bandits are waiting for dark to move in, and obviously a handful of simple village folk are not about to stop 'em!''

Lansford went on bitching as he lightly sketched in the outlaw lines around San Mateo. The map scale was too small to go into details Lansford didn't know, anyway. But the old infantryman remembered enough I and R to add a thoughtful *X* and say, ''This looks like their command post, out here a quarter mile southwest of the village under some trees that ain't on this map. They've got their horses remudad up there, with an asshole red flag of some kind waving in the trades. Why do bandit chiefs like red flags so much?''

''Maybe they think they're bullfighters. How come they're not covering this stream bed looping around the east wall of the village, Dutch?''

''It's not a stream bed. It's a son of a bitching deep arroyo. They can't hit San Mateo from that direction and San Mateo can't get *away* that way, either. The cliffs are steep as hell. The old Spanish dons obviously built there in the first place because of the arroyo protecting at least one corner of the place from wild Injuns.''

Captain Gringo studied the map thoughtfully as he said,

"The Spanish conquistadores weren't afraid of Indians. It was the other way around. I'd say they planted San Mateo next to an arroyo with flat fertile soil all around because they needed water, like everyone else. There has to be at least one footpath the village women use to go down the cliffs to get water from the bottom of this arroyo, Dutch.''

Lansford shrugged and said, "If you say so. We didn't get a look at that side of town. We scouted the situation from this wooded ridge, *here,* then ran home to Mother as soon as we had it figured. That same ridge would screen us nicely from the whole mess if we just went on south, *this* way. Can't we please do that, Mommy? Those other kids down the block look awfully rough for nice girls like us to play with.''

Captain Gringo chuckled, but said, "There may be some nice girls in that village who don't want to play with them after dark, either. Okay, it's going on high noon, and the village is only about five miles away on the map. We'll make it during la siesta, easily.''

Lansford looked uneasy as he asked, "Make *what,* for chrissake? Sure, we outnumber the sons of bitches and have them outgunned. But our side took casualties even at Wounded Knee, Dick! There's no way anyone can take out five hundred armed men without at least a few of them shooting back pretty good, and that whole fucking village isn't worth a flesh wound we're not being paid to accept!''

Captain Gringo spotted Gaston headed their way with a curious expression on his face. So he stood and called out, "Gaston, you're in command until I get back. I'm taking one Maxim and a rifle platoon out to see what we can do about some uncouth types. Dutch here can explain the basic situation to you, if you *give* a shit. I'm running against the clock and I have to get cracking.''

He turned away, made his way through the trees to the nearest machine-gun section, and told them to pick up the Maxim and follow him. Then he turned the other way to look for a rifle platoon too dumb to make themselves scarce during a trail break. Dutch Lansford had already pulled one out for him from his own company and was packing his own Krag as he saluted mockingly and said, "Ready when you are, Napoleon."

Captain Gringo nodded and kept walking as Dutch fell in on his left, with the others trailing behind. He asked the old infantryman, "How come you're so eager all of a sudden, Dutch? I thought you didn't think it was worth the risk?"

Lansford shrugged and said, "I don't. But I'm never going to get a wink of sleep until I see how you mean to pull it off. So I may as well come along and watch!"

"That's what I like, a sentimental slob who worries about women and children. But if you're so anxious to save the world, we may as well do it right. I need another officer with me like I need a nagging wife. What say you do something useful instead? If Gaston holds the fort here with the main body and you take, oh, a company or so out to hold that wooded ridge overlooking the village and surrounding milpas, we'd have the pricks in a pincers, see?"

Lansford looked dubiously back at the small force Captain Gringo was taking with him to do whatever and observed, "You sure are one optimistic son of a bitch, Dick. But what the hell, let's *do* it."

There was plenty of time to lay out the plan for his few followers as Captain Gringo led them in a wide detour through rugged wooded country to approach San Mateo the hard way. So they were considerably relieved to discover that they hadn't "volunteered" for a suicide mission after all. Just a scary one.

They reached the arroyo well north of the village, where the banks were neither as steep nor as deep, and still had a time getting themselves and the machine gun with its ammo down to the water's edge.

The ever-deepening arroyo drained south, and in the dry

season, the stream that had carved it patiently over the years through layers of volcanic ash and rock was only ankle deep. This was just as well, since there was nowhere else to walk down there.

When they finally spotted the blue tiles of the San Mateo bell tower looming high above them over the rim of the arroyo, the sergeant next in command under Captain Gringo nudged him and murmured, "I am sorry. I make no excuses for my nervous condition, Captain Gringo. But has it occurred to you that any bandito peeking over from up there has us at considerable disadvantage?"

Captain Gringo answered, "Many many times, Alverado. Would you like to be excused for the rest of the afternoon?"

"Gracias, no. Alas, I do not have the courage to behave like a coward at times like this. I get in more trouble that way!"

Captain Gringo laughed, then stopped and raised his hand to say, "Bueno, muchachos. As we hoped, there *is* a path cut into the cliff ahead. From here on it gets tricky. Sergeant Alverado, hold everyone here and be ready for sudden moves should anyone get trigger-happy. I'd better go on up alone and tell 'em we're not bad guys before they even *see* that machine gun. Who's got a big white pocket kerchief?"

Alverado produced one and held it out, but as Captain Gringo took it with a nod of thanks, Alverado asked, "What if you get shot on the way up, Captain Gringo?"

"I'll doubtless come back down faster, dead. If that happens, you're to get yourself and the others out of here pronto. There's no sense in being silly about a rescue mission if the people don't want to be rescued, right?"

"The thought had occurred to me before now, Captain Gringo. For why are you risking your life for strangers? You owe those villagers up there nothing. They are not even your people. I just don't understand you!"

"Lots of people have told me that. Keep your eye on the birdie. Here goes nothing."

As his men watched nervously, Captain Gringo moved

alone down the arroyo, feeling not a little nervous himself, and held up the dirty white kerchief as he started up the footpath. There was of course no guardrail, and the narrow ledge had been intended from the beginning for the smaller feet of women and children fetching water. As if that weren't enough to worry about, as he rose high enough to sincerely hope he didn't slip, a gruff voice from above shouted down, "I have you in my sights, you big defiler of your own mother's grave!"

Captain Gringo waved the improvised truce flag as he stopped to call back, "I should *hope* you'd have someone covering this path, Señor. May I come up and explain myself?"

"For why? I am sure I can hit you from here, and I do not converse socially with ladrón fuckers of pigs and chickens!"

"I'm sure you could nail me easily, Amigo. But then you'd have no idea what I was up to, and you know, of course, you haven't a chance of holding them off once it gets dark?"

"*Them*, you say? Are you not with those other ladrónes?"

"Now would I be standing here like an asshole armed with a kerchief if I meant to attack a whole village in broad daylight?"

"You could be loco en la cabeza. But come on up and we'll hear you out. I warn you, this had better be good!"

Apparently they thought it was, once he'd joined the cluster of anxious-looking armed farmers at the top of the cliff and explained who he was and what he had in mind. It paid to advertise, and Captain Gringo was well known in Costa Rica as a peaceful resident of San José when he wasn't off killing Colombians, Nicaraguans, and other vermin. The old village priest, in command of the defenses since the village alcalde had been killed in the first confusion early that morning, got everyone else to shut up so he could ask Captain Gringo just what he wanted them all to do.

He said, "First we get my men and machine gun up out

of the arroyo, Padre. By the way, do you have people here related to the Castro family in San José?''

The older man said he didn't think so. Captain Gringo didn't want to curse in front of a fatherly priest. So he just sighed and moved back to the arroyo rim to wave his men and materiel on up. As they waited for them to climb the treacherous path with the Maxim, Captain Gringo told the priest, ''I'm going up in your bell tower, with your permission, for a bird's-eye, Padre. Have my men join me there, por favor.''

Then, without waiting for an answer, he was legging it through the village to do just what he'd said. The ''village streets'' were a maze of narrow unpaved lanes, which seemed reasonable, cluttered with kids, pigs, and other innocent bystanders, which did not. As he strode along, keeping his bearing on the one tower rising above everything else, he bellowed, ''Get everybody that's not packing a gun under cover, you poor stupid bastards! Haven't you ever been under siege before?''

They must not have. A couple of women came out to scoop up babies. But other villagers came to their doorways to stare blankly at him, as if he'd just come down from the moon in a big balloon. He grimaced and went on, singing under his breath, ''As I go walking down the street, the people from their doorsteps holler, there goes that Protestant son of a bitch, the one who shagged O'Reilly's daughter!''

It looked even worse from high up in the bell tower.

From his vantage point in the sky among the old bronze bells and bat shit, Captain Gringo wondered how on earth the village had lasted this long. The irregular stucco-over-adobe walls below were less than a dozen feet high and lightly manned by a straw hat and hunting rifle every fifty feet or more. Out across the corn and bean milpas all around there were *other* straw hats, a hell of a lot of straw hats, that probably couldn't be seen from their angle by the pathetically few villagers on the walls. There was no mystery as to why the villagers hadn't thought to send at

least one lookout up here until now. The bandits doubtless
had them down as simple villagers, too. They just didn't
have the guts to rush even farmers led by an unarmed
priest in broad daylight.

He didn't wonder what the outlaws were after. Even the
smallest Hispanic church had at least a little gold in the
form of easily portable altar service, and some of the
village girls down there were sort of pretty.

He spotted the distant red flag Dutch Lansford had
mentioned. Things looked slightly different on the scene
than on thc map. They always did. But he had his bearings
now. That gentle tree-covered rise beyond the fields to the
west-northwest would be the tree-covered ridge Dutch had
mentioned. If Dutch hadn't changed his mind, he'd have
made it there by now, having less distance to cover. So it
was better than fifty-fifty that the bandits out there had
rifles trained on their asses they didn't know about. If their
chief jerking off over there to the west had the brains to
send out scouts, he'd have known better than to start this
bullshit in the first place. There wasn't enough loot, or
even ass, in the whole village for a band that size to bother
with. He wondered who in the hell they could be. Costa
Rica didn't have a large bandit population. It was tough to
keep self-styled Robin Hoods in the field when the country
people were content under a reasonable government.

Nothing much seemed to be going on as the siesta-time
sun rose ever higher and the people on both sides below
realized they were up past their usual bedtimes. Then
someone on the walls below made a dumb move and a
machine gun tap-danced slugs along the top of the wall his
hat had shown above for a minute. Captain Gringo stared
grimly at the blue haze of smoke drifting from a corner
clump of brush along the bandit skirmish line and muttered,
"Thanks, motherfucker. I was *wondering* where you were!"

He wondered where they'd gotten the automatic weapon, too. One of the reasons his services were so in demand
down here was that most Latin Americans didn't have or
know how to use the recently invented machine gun.

Automatic weapons used expensive amounts of ammo, even when used right. The jerk-off out there in that clump was using his as a glorified sniper's rifle. Ergo, they'd somehow picked up a machine gun nobody in the bunch really knew how to use.

He turned from the narrow opening when he heard Alverado coming up the ladder, coughing and spitting. As the sergeant's head appeared, Captain Gringo smiled and said, "Those bats sure shit a lot for such little critters, don't they? Where's the Maxim?"

"Below, in the nave, Captain Gringo. Do you wish for to have it up *here?*"

"Why, no, I thought I'd just ring the *bells* for the bastards! Get it up here, dammit, with plenty of ammo, poco tiempo!"

Alverado turned on the ladder to roar orders down even more rudely, and that seemed to be the answer to getting heavy weapons up a ladder in a hurry. Captain Gringo told his crew how he wanted the Maxim set up and, as they worked at it, told Alverado to go down and tell the priest to tell his people to just sit tight and not get overeager, adding, "It's dumb to get killed chasing armed men through tall corn, no matter how fast they seem to be running away, and they may never have heard of a counterattack. You'd better stay with the padre and command the walls. Tell the riflemen with us not to go chasing after medals, either, and—oh shit, *you* know what to do. So go *do* it!"

Alverado grinned proudly, nodded, and went down to play Travis at the Alamo, albeit hopefully the *smart* way.

By this time the Maxim squatted on its tripod, armed and dangerous, with its steel snout dominating the chosen field of fire. So Captain Gringo dropped to his knees behind the breech and explained to his interested spectators, "There's a time to brace a Maxim on one's hip and play cowboy. This ain't it. The main skirmish line is just within range, even from up here. So watch Teacher and

I'll show you how to draw a dotted line with the traverse screw.''

He pulled the arming lever to seat the first round in the chamber, then saw, when a live round popped out to roll across the guano-flecked floorboards, that there'd already been one ready to fire, and growled, ''Shame on you, Rosario. Don't ever do that again.''

Then, before the embarrassed gunner could answer, Captain Gringo pulled the trigger and they all jumped halfway out of their skins as the heavy machine gun's deep-throated roar filled the bell tower with ear-ringing echos.

Captain Gringo's first point of aim was of course the other side's machine-gun nest. He saw he was firing a little over. So he stopped to depress his sights with the elevation knob, giving the other machine-gun crew a chance to fire back.

They, of course, could climb the bell tower only halfway with their return fire from that distance and lower position. But their gunsmoke haze made a handy target, and the smoke was soon joined by confetti clouds of chopped-up shrubbery and whoever was behind it as Captain Gringo zeroed a long, withering burst into their position.

Then since the skirmish line to the south was longer and had a better escape route, he methodically traversed down it, his dotted line of hot lead punctuated by flying hats, rifles twirling high in the air, and an occasional figure who simply bolted and ran before the deadly fire reached him. Captain Gringo left them for his riflemen below to deal with, and Alverado and his boys dealt with them just fine.

The Krag was a good rifle, even when it wasn't being fired with both elbows braced over a wall. One could almost feel sorry for a poor bastard floundering in panic through a muddy corn milpa with .30-30 rounds plucking away at the strings of his life, if one could forget just what kind of a bastard he *was!* At least none of the bandits had to suffer rape, torture, or both, before a bullet snuffed out his lamp forever.

Some of the outlaws on the remaining north flank seemed to be quick learners. By the time Captain Gringo had reloaded with a fresh belt and was traversing their positions, most of them were off and running, fast, for the apparent safe cover of the tree-lined ridge to the west-northwest. Alverado and the others below accounted for a goodly number of them before they'd run out of range. But most seemed to be getting away. It depended on whether Dutch Lansford and his own forces were waiting for them in the trees over that way, and if Dutch had brought along enough help to stop what still looked to be about a hundred or more coming at him, still armed and obviously upset about something, if all that yelling and cowboy shooting meant anything.

Dutch had. Everyone in the besieged village had stopped firing by now. So it was easy to make out the crackle of small-arms' fire as the fleeing survivors ran or, from Lansford's position, charged into rifle range of the tree line. The villagers below burst into cheers as ladrón after ladrón proceeded to do amusing cartwheels, backflips, or simply gave good imitations of punctured balloons while Lansford's people punctured them indeed.

Some few hit the dirt or dropped to one knee to fire back blindly into the trees. None of them lasted long, and it didn't help when the last few dropped their weapons and just stood there, hands held high as they pleaded for their lives. A guy standing still like that made a *really* neat target.

As the last of them were going down, Captain Gringo shot a wistful look at the outlaw command post, out of everybody's range. The red flag still fluttered. He couldn't tell at this range just what was going on over there, but from all the dust, it figured the head bandit and his court were mounting up to go someplace, anyplace, in a hurry. Captain Gringo sighed and said, ''Oh, well, you can't win 'em all.''

Then the red flag and everything around it vanished in a

big fat ball of smoke and flame, followed by another, and another, as fast as a mountain mortar could be reloaded!

As the shock waves tingled the old bells behind him, Captain Gringo said, "Why, thank you, Gaston. That was very considerate of you. But who in hell is minding the store?"

As it turned out, nobody was. When Captain Gringo saw that the situation was under control, if not over, he told his crew to manhandle the Maxim down from the bell tower and then beat them to the bottom.

It was a little tough getting to the village gate, with all those people either trying to beat his back black and blue, kiss him to orgasm, or get him drunk, all at the same time. But he finally made it without having to pull his .38 on anyone. As he strode out across the killing ground, followed like the Pied Piper by half the village or more, he spotted Dutch and Gaston coming across from the ridge to meet him. It was nice to see that his own people had enough sense to hold their positions until an official fiesta was declared, at least.

He waved back and pointed as he swerved to make for the erstwhile ladrón command post, with them swerving to intercept him that way. He wasn't too concerned about the occasional body he passed, sprawled across the killing ground. One dead shit heel looked much like another. The remains of their leaders might tell him something he didn't know already.

They did. He met Gaston and Dutch a few yards from the craters Gaston's skilled gunnery had left, and when the three of them got closer they could hear someone moaning. Dutch said, "I'll be damned. One of 'em must still be breathing."

Gaston reached into his jacket for his own .38 as he muttered, "Merde alors, I must be getting rusty. But I can fix that, hein?"

Captain Gringo snapped, "Hold the thought until we see what he has to say for himself, dammit. Dutch, what are the casualty figures for *our* side?"

Lansford said, "Light. We took a few hits. Nobody killed. We would have taken less, had not some of the green kids and adelitas jumped up to cheer a little early."

"Bueno. We can leave our wounded here with the villagers, then. I think they like us."

He saw the red flag draped over the lip of a shell crater ahead. The moaning was coming from the other side of the shallow but serious excavation. He said, "Gaston, your fuses are set too long for shrapnel," and Gaston said a dreadful thing about his mother.

He chuckled and picked up the flag as Gaston grumbled, "I know shrapnel's supposed to go off above ground level. My *boys* know shrapnel is supposed to go off above ground level, but do the triple-titted toads who made the *fuses* know what the fuck they are doing?"

Captain Gringo held out the flag to Gaston and said, "What the fuck indeed! Does this rag look familiar to you, Gaston?"

Gaston stared soberly at the red flag's emblem of a Latin cross superimposed on the scales of justice and said, "Oui, but I was hoping we'd *wiped out* those lunatics we met in Panama that time!"

Dutch asked them what they were talking about, of course, so Captain Gringo said, "Half-assed Utopian rebels calling themselves Los Jurados. Get Gaston to tell you. I have to see what I can get out of the Jurado we didn't wipe out after all."

He circled the crater to find a heavyset mestizo wearing a once fancy blue uniform. He and his costume were both torn up bad. The guts were ripped open by shrapnel, but the face was still recognizable. The tall American hunkered down beside the dying man and said, "Hello, Pablo. I'm surprised to meet up with you again, here in Costa Rica."

Pablo opened his eyes, smiled wanly, and replied, "I am surprised and *sorry,* I think, to see *you* again. I might have known when I heard the dulcet tones of a Maxim fired by a professional. It *was* you, of course, who made mincemeat out of me and mine just now, Captain Gringo?"

"I'm afraid so, Pablo. Nothing personal."

"Would you have held your fire had you known I was an old comrade in arms, Yanqui?"

"Not really. The last time we spoke, after smoking up Los Jurados together, you neglected to tell us you intended to carry on their mission, whatever the hell it is."

"Hey, Gringo, I spit on the mission of those sissy-boy rebels! By the balls of Santiago, I am a *real* rebel. Or I was, until just now. What did you get me with, a mortar?"

"Yeah. I see you kept that machine gun I had to leave behind as well as the banner and other trimmings of Los Jurados. If I asked, polite, would you tell me if you jumped the border to go into business for yourself, or did someone send you?"

Pablo tried to laugh, gargled blood instead, and asked, "What could you do to make a dying man talk, Captain Gringo, *hurt* him?"

"Naturally. Even a guy in your condition has *feelings*, right?"

"Hey, don't get nasty with old war comrades, you big bastard. Can't you take a joke? I told you when we kissed good-bye down south I was going into the revolución business for to do it right. Nobody told me where to go or what to do. I, Pablo, have always done as I fucking pleased, eh?"

That sounded reasonable, and Captain Gringo didn't have to ask why the burly bandit had seen fit to attack an innocent village. So he said, "Look, Pablo, if there's anyone you want us to get in touch with for you, or anything you want to say . . ."

Then he waved his hand before the dead eyes staring up at him and got back to his feet with a shrug.

As the others joined him, he said, "I'd do it again if I had to, and knowing *him*, I'd *have* to. But it sure feels odd, now that I know at least some of those guys we killed out there in the corn fought on our side, *good*, the time we took out Los Jurados."

Gaston shrugged and said, "Those are the fortunes of war, when one is a soldier of fortune, non?"

Captain Gringo repressed a shudder and turned to Lansford to say, "Okay, we've enjoyed all the fun parts. Now it's the time to clean up. Just who were the people on our side who got hit, Dutch?"

Lansford rattled off a short list of Latin names, ending with, "Oh, yeah, and that sexy adelita, Azucar. She's the one who got it the worst. Keyhole wound in the tummy. She still might make it, given a good medic."

But Captain Gringo wasn't listening. He was off and running. Dutch looked at Gaston and asked, "Jesus, what did I just say?" and, since Captain Gringo seldom bragged about his love life, even to Gaston, Gaston could only answer, "It beats the merde out of me, too."

It wasn't hard to locate Azucar up on the tree-covered ridge. All the adelitas and far too many soldados were gathered around her as she lay on a blanket spread on the forest duff. The other wounded were attracting less attention than they probably wanted, since it wasn't hard to tell Azucar was dying, either.

They didn't have anything like a qualified wound surgeon within miles, and, even if they'd had, it was doubtful if even the best Victorian doctors could have saved her. Where the optimistic Dutch had gotten the idea anyone could take a ricocheting rifle slug through the guts, and live, was a total mystery. Captain Gringo knew, as soon as he'd bulled through the crowd and knelt to examine her, she was dead. But he didn't think she'd want to hear that. So he didn't tell her. He simply roared, "All right, everybody *back*, God damn it, and give us some light on the subject! You, there, Frutos, you're supposed to be an officer. Act like one. This is supposed to be a combat outfit, not a gaggle of geese!"

That worked as far as the men went. Some of the adelitas even moved off to tend to their camp chores.

But a lot of them didn't, and little Maria was being a particular pest as she sat on her knees at his side, pleading with him to do something for her friend. So he said, "All right, I need hot water. Lots of hot water. Go put lots of pots on, and, oh yeah, take some of these dames *with* you!"

Azucar was trying to say something. So as Maria scampered off to be helpful, Captain Gringo bent to put his ear near the dying girl's still-lush lips. She whispered, "They pulled my skirts up for to see where I was hurt, Deek. Can anyone see my pussy?"

"Don't worry about it. It's the prettiest little pussy in the world."

"It is *your* pussy, Deek. I will never forget how I gave it to you, completely."

That was a safe bet, since it would be a miracle if she lasted until sundown. But his voice was gentle as he said, "*I'll* never forget it, either. Try to breath shallower, Azucar."

"I can't. I have to inhale all I can, and it still does not feel like I am getting any air. Am I...dying, Deek?"

"Don't talk dumb. It's just a scratch. Just try to relax and we'll see about a compress or whatever before we carry you into the village."

He started to straighten up for another look at her shot-up naked guts. But she reached one hand up to hold him, weakly, as she pleaded, "Do not move your face away from mine, Querido. I am having so much trouble for to see you as it is. Is the sun going down or something like that?"

"Yeah, sure, something like that. These trees cast a lot of shade."

She sighed and murmured, "Bueno, it feels much better now that the cool shades of evening envelop us. It is getting a little *too* cool, in fact, for to lie naked under the stars alone. Why don't we make love some more for to warm our flesh, Querido?"

He said, "Not just yet, por favor. I need to get my second wind with a mujer like you, see?"

She smiled wanly, and he thanked God her voice was too soft to carry as she murmured, "I am glad you enjoy my body so much. You have such a lovely body, Deek. But would you please not thrust quite so *deeply*, until I get used to that big thing of yours? I'm sorry, I am trying to respond to you, Deek, but tonight it *hurts* for some reason and, oh, *no*, por favor! I can't take it up the *ass* so deep. Won't you take it out of there and do it the old-fashioned way, just this once? No, no, for God's sake, Deek, you are *hurting* me inside!"

He tried to hold her still as she writhed in pain, trying to soothe her with lying words of endearment that she probably didn't understand in her delirium. She started to struggle harder. Then something inside her popped like a bubble, she tried to scream, but vomited blood and bile instead, and then mercifully it was over.

As he closed her dead eyes with gentle, nostalgic fingertips, he heard a familiar voice behind him call out, "Where do you wish for us to set all this hot water, Deek?"

He turned with a puzzled frown to see little Maria and another girl lugging what looked like a steaming cannibal pot between them and growled, "Hot water? What in the fuck would I do with hot water? Oh, yeah, right. Put it right down there, muchachas."

They did so. Then Maria came closer to drop to her knees at his side by the dead girl, and asked, "How is she, Deek? She looks like she is more comfortable now. But she's messed herself very much, at both ends. Is that for why you wanted so much hot water?"

Actually, like many a country doctor back home, he'd put people to work boiling water to get them out of his hair for the moment. But all he told Maria was, "She's as comfortable as she'll ever be, now. We'd better let the water cool a bit before we wash the corpse and roll it up in that blanket."

"Oh, *no!*" Maria sobbed. "She can't be *dead!*"

He shrugged and said, "Sure she can. It's easy. Staying *alive* is the only part that's *hard*."

For a spur-of-the-moment fiesta it was pisser. So Captain Gringo knew he'd probably have some drunks if not deserters to worry about in the cold gray dawn. But meanwhile his people had earned a little fun as well as the undying gratitude of San Mateo. So he let them whoop it up as he made his way more sedately to the church.

There, as he'd hoped, he found the old priest dining alone in the rectory instead of out getting screwed blewed and tattooed like everyone else in town.

The fatherly father sat him down at the old oaken table and insisted he at least have some wine, explaining, as he poured, "I gave my servants the night off. Alas, I expect to spend a lot of time in the confessional this coming Saturday."

Captain Gringo smiled simpático, raised his wine goblet in a silent toast, and said, "I'm not sure we could call this visit a confession, Padre. For one thing, I'm not of your faith."

The older man resumed his own seat, smiled gently, and said, "When a person comes to me with a troubled soul, my son, I am not required by the Church to dispute theology. My task is for to offer comfort and advice if it is in my power. I am, as you can see, but an ignorant country priest."

"You don't look ignorant to me, Padre, and I *do* have some problems you might be able to help me with."

"I shall try, my son. What is it you wish for to confess?"

Captain Gringo grimaced and replied, "I try not to do things I should be ashamed of, Padre. I suppose in the eyes of your church or any other I'm a sinner. But I'll take that up with the guy upstairs when and if I have to."

The old priest nodded soberly and said, "Perhaps the

world would be a better place if there were more sinners like you, my son. Even here in this remote village we have heard the tales of Captain Gringo. If half of them are true, I greatly fear for your immortal soul. On the other hand, I greatly fear for the immortal souls of many who attend Mass more regularly. Now, in what way may I be of service to you?"

Captain Gringo sipped his mellow Madeira thoughtfully before he said, "You know one of our adelitas was killed today, and you know, of course, what an adelita is."

The priest nodded and said, "I also run this parish. Naturally the unfortunate young woman will be laid to rest in hallowed ground, with the full rites of the faith she may or may not have strayed from."

Captain Gringo swallowed and said, "Thank you, Padre. I'm sure that was more than she might have expected, and it's very generous of you."

The gentle old true gentleman looked sincerely bemused as he shrugged and replied, "For why do I deserve thanks just for doing my duty? Is there anything *else* I can do for you or your people, my son?"

"Well, hopefully no more of *my* outfit will require a proper funeral, if I can get them out of here soon enough. But, look, I know those dead outlaws killed people of this village, and would have done worse things had they won. They no doubt deserve the mass burial your guys gave them out on the edges of your cleared land. But, you see, down in Panama a while back, at least some of them fought on the side of the angels, or at least they fought pretty good against people even worse than they were. Obviously my old comrade, Pablo, went from bad to just plain vicious since the last time we met, but, I dunno, it just seems wrong, to me at least, to just let 'em rot without *saying* anything about it."

The old priest was staring at him with an odd expression, and Captain Gringo braced himself for a gentle tirade on the wages of sin. Instead, the older man nodded and said, "There is not room in our churchyard for so many graves, even if they'd died in a state of grace. But would it suffice for you if I simply read a Mass over them, where they lie tonight?''

Captain Gringo nodded soberly and replied, "It would more than suffice, Padre. No offense, but you're a hell of a gent.''

"Thank you. I take that as a compliment, coming from you, my son. I am ashamed to confess, however, the thought had not occurred to me before you reminded me of my duties to even lapsed Catholics. So it is I who should thank *you*. I only wish I could do *more* for you, my son.''

Captain Gringo said, "I do have one last favor to ask. But it may be too hard a row to hoe, even for you, Padre. Now that we've done all anyone can for the dead, I've got one living and very messed-up teen-ager on my hands who's in an awful mess.''

"I would be happy to hear her confession, Captain Gringo.''

"That's the crazy part, Padre. The poor kid hasn't got anything *to* confess. Not yet, anyway, but you know what they say about adelitas, and most of what they say is true.''

"I am sorry, forgive me, but I find this conversation most confusing, my son. If the child is, as you say, innocent of any sin, for why would she need the services of an unworldly village priest?''

Captain Gringo sighed and said, "It's a long story.'' Then he told it to the old priest, leaving out nothing but a few dirty words, and even so, the poor old guy looked pretty shocked.

When Captain Gringo had brought him up-to-date on Maria Castro, the old priest nodded soberly and said, "I believe you. For I know the kind of man you are. The wicked young harlot who caused all the trouble will no doubt answer in Hell for the trouble she caused. Meanwhile, her young innocent victim hopefully has a lifetime in the here and now ahead of her, and I agree we must prevent her from spending it as a fallen woman. But, alas,

I could probably do more for a fallen woman than I could to convince such a father that his suspicions are without foundation! Oh, my, if only you had brought me a simple problem like a lapsed heretic or habitual criminal. I have been instructed by His Holiness in Rome how to deal with *them!*"

He sipped his wine as Captain Gringo said, "I'm stuck, too, Padre. We thought she might have someone here in San Mateo who might be able to help her, but . . ."

"Oh, I assure you she *has*," the priest cut in.

So Captain Gringo brightened and asked, "Oh? You've located the cousins she said she might have here, Padre?"

The old priest sighed and said, "One of them. Laid to rest several years ago in the churchyard. After you'd asked about the family, I of course examined our parish records. The head of the household died of vomito negro. The widow left soon after, with the children. They left no forwarding address. Maria Castro has no living relatives in San Mateo."

"But you said there was someone here who would help her and . . . Oh, sorry, dumb question. But how are you going to convince her family back in San José, Padre?"

The older man shrugged and said, "Quién sabe? I can only try. I shall write to my brother priest of their parish, in code as well as Latin, of course. We don't want her overwrought father doing anything silly if even his church can't calm him down. Meanwhile, the girl shall be safe here in the arms of the True Faith."

Captain Gringo looked dubious and said, "I don't know, Padre. I'm sure the kid's still a virgin, but I just can't see her as a *nun*, for some reason."

The old priest laughed in a surprisingly boyish manner and replied, "That might be overdoing things. Since you told me she made a habit of running off to join guerrilla armies, she may be a bit overactive to consider a life of devotion just yet. I mean to keep her here, with me, in the rectory, and please don't wonder aloud if the stories our enemies tell about priests and their housekeepers are true. I assure you such events take place less often than Martin Luther suspected, and in any case, I am too old for that sort of nonsense.''

Captain Gringo laughed and said truthfully, ''That thought hadn't crossed my mind. But I thought you already *had* servants here, Padre.''

''A properly run Hispanic household can always find room for an extra pair of willing hands. The old battle-ax who is usually in charge of the others, and who should be ashamed for displaying her ankles at the fiesta at her age, will see that Maria will be kept busy and out of trouble with the village gallants until such time as God gives me the wisdom to find a more permanent solution. Meanwhile, she will be safe and well supervised with us, no?''

Captain Gringo nodded gratefully and said, ''I don't know what your church pays you, Padre, but it's not enough.''

''I think it is. Would you like some more Madeira, my son?''

''I would, but no, thanks, Padre. Now that I've solved some of my more pressing problems, thanks to you, I have to get back to work on the ones I have left.''

As he rose, the old priest asked, ''Are you sure there is nothing more I can do for you, my son?''

Captain Gringo said, ''Not unless you know more than I think you should about fieldstripping and cleaning machine guns, Padre.''

They marched on the next morning, leaving Maria and their just-as-useless dead and wounded behind in San Mateo. They hadn't lost many people and they'd gained on arms, ammo, and supplies that Pablo's gang had been packing. So things were looking up.

The machine gun the outlaws had mistreated all the way up from Panama was in a disgraceful state. But it was not beyond repair, and Captain Gringo figured he had to have something to do with his hands during trail breaks, now that he'd given up women for a while. Few of the outlaws' guns had been worth packing along, since everyone in the outfit already had newer and better Krags to begin with. But the ubiquitous .30-30 rounds the ladrónes had been loading their motley antiques with more than made up for the ammo expended in wiping out the band. So Captain Gringo told Gaston to stop bitching about the few mortar rounds he was short of now, adding that they'd probably be able to pick up more at the border post they still had to pass before they might need them.

Gaston never stopped bitching unless he was eating out a woman or in some other kind of trouble. So he said, "Merde alors, who is to say when a growing boy might need artillery rounds? Were you expecting to meet Los Jurados again, on either side of the très fuzzy border?"

They were marching at the head of the column with Dutch Lansford at the moment. So while Captain Gringo just snorted in disgust and didn't answer, Dutch asked, "Just who in hell are these Jurados you guys are expecting to meet up with again? Those guys back there just looked like shit-house bandits to me."

Before Gaston could find a soapbox, Captain Gringo said, "I'll tell him, Gaston. You take an hour to say what time it is," adding, for the other soldier of fortune's information, "Pablo and his gang back there weren't the real thing. Hopefully there aren't many of the real thing left. They were a band of fanatics the Spanish Inquisition missed. A leftover branch of the crusading Knights Templars, so crazy the Knights Templars disowned them."

Dutch frowned and asked, "And they were still running around loose, this late in the 1800s?"

"What can I tell you? Hispanic culture's a little slow catching up. Anyhow, the bunch we tangled with a while back, back where we're going, were led by a crazy old asshole I *know* we killed. But some of them might have gotten away in the confusion."

"How do you tell the real thing from a bandit? They all act like crazy bastards."

"For one thing, Los Jurados are a celibate order of fighting monks. To keep themselves pure, they submit to voluntary castration."

Dutch walked on in silence for a moment as he pondered that, then said, "When you're right you're right. They *must* be nuts! Okay, I'll tell my scouts to keep their eyes peeled for nutless lunatics, and they say the Colombian army can act a little wild, too."

Captain Gringo shrugged and said, "They're just doing their job. Colombia still owns the isthmus of Panama, rebels and Tío Sam permitting. The Colombian military junta wants more than anyone's willing to pay for the dubious fun of completing that Panama Canal the French gave up on a few years back. So rebels find it surprisingly easy to get guns in Panama. Which is why we're supposed to keep this season's revolution on that side of the border, if we can. There are dozens of half-assed rebel factions, good guys and bad guys, swapping shots with the Colombian regulars, and our employers want the Colombian *regulars* to stay the hell out of their country, too. So forget about Los Jurados. We'll have plenty of targets where we're going, with or without balls!"

Dutch turned to Gaston and asked, "Is he always this cheerful?"

Gaston said, "Wait until he gets us up in a balloon or in another armored horseless carriage, Dutch. That is when you'll *really* see how insane the idiot can be!"

Captain Gringo glanced up at the sun and said, "The open ground up ahead and that noonday sun overhead add up to a trail break in these woods, guys. May as well let the adelitas cook warm rations while we wait out the sunstroke hours. We might have to feast on cold rations a lot once we're in enemy territory."

They halted the column and split up to give the right orders. Captain Gringo got his end of camp in order and moved deeper into the highland slash pines to take a leak and try to think without people buzzing in his ears like flies. He had a lot to think about.

He came to an unexpected little mountain stream purring softly over polished pebbles and sat down in the lush green streamside grass to remove his hat and boots. He tossed the hat on the nearby grass and tossed his bare feet in the cool caressing water as he fumbled in his shirt pocket for a smoke. He cursed softly when he found he'd smoked the last of the claros he'd transferred from the box in the supply wagon to his shirt that morning. His ass and feet felt too good right now to get up and go back for more. So he plucked a sweet grass stem to chew, and the hell with it.

He took out his map, noted that it had nothing new to tell him, and put it away. At the rate they were going, nothing exciting promised to happen before they reached the small border outpost and the bridge across the deep canyon running more or less in line with the border. They figured to reach both within forty-eight hours, if he could keep his people out of trouble and just keep 'em picking 'em up and laying 'em down as the trail kept getting steeper.

He heard movement behind him and turned to see a small dark girl with Indian features and waist-length hair approaching shyly with a tray of tortillas, rice, and beans, along with a canteen cup of coffee.

She sank shyly to her knees beside him with the goodies in her lap as she murmured, "I knew you might be hungry, Captain Gringo, so I took the liberty of bringing you some refrescos. I am called Angelica."

He smiled and said, "They named you right, Angeli-ca," as he took the goodies from her lap, trying to resist speculations on what other goodies the pretty little mestiza might have in her lap under that print peon skirt.

She was free to leave now if she wanted to. So he couldn't help wondering why she wanted to stay, watching him wolf down the simple hearty fare. The coffee was good, too. So he asked her if she'd made it, and she blushed a dusky shade of rose and nodded modestly when he told her it was muy bueno. When he'd drained the cup and refilled it from the sparkling stream to wash down the last of her "Moors and Christians," she looked anxious and asked if he wanted her to run and fetch him more coffee. He said, "No, thanks. Have you eaten, Angelica?"

She said, "Sí, while I was stirring the pot. I am, as anyone can see, too fat as it is, no?"

She was obviously fishing for compliments. Like most mestizas of Guaymi blood on the Costa Rican Indian side, Angelica was a little chunky but firmly built under her tawny smooth skin. The Spanish side of her family tree had added some more-familiar curves to her solid little figure. He laughed and said, "You're pretty as a picture and you know it, Angelica. Whose adelita are you, by the way? If he's bigger than me, we shouldn't be talking this way."

She'd been waiting for such an opening. He'd surmised as much. So he wasn't too astounded when she sighed and said, "I am *nobody's* mujer now, alas. My soldado ran away, even before the battle we fought back there."

"Oh? I'm sorry to hear that, Angelica."

"I am not. I did not think he was much of a man, even before he proved himself a coward."

Captain Gringo placed the cup and tray well out of the way in the grass as he said, "I'm beginning to understand your problem. You want permission to head back to San José, right?"

She sighed, shook her head, and said, "Pero no, gracias. There is nothing back there for me but a father who beats me and desires me for to be a servant when he is not molesting me. I much prefer this life of adventure, if you will have me."

He raised an eyebrow and asked, "In what sense do you mean that, Angelica? As a free woman attached to this expedition or what?"

"What," she replied, staring down at the grass between them as she added, "It is not healthy for men and women to sin against nature in their lonely sleeping rolls, I think, and you left your own adelita behind at that village. So, if you will have me . . .''

He grinned and said, "Oh, Angelica, this is so sudden."

She pouted her most kissable little lips and pleaded, "Please do not mock me, Captain Gringo. I am not very witty and I always lose when people mock me. For I do not know how to mock them back."

He said, "I'm not laughing at you. I'm laughing at me."

She smiled with radiant relief and said, "Oh, *you* are not funny. You are most bravo y hermoso! I know *I* am something for to laugh at. Some of my ancestors ran about naked in the jungle, according to the neighbors. But if you do not find me *too* ugly . . .''

"That's not the problem and you know it," he cut in, explaining, "A commanding officer has to be careful who he favors, Angelica. You don't look like you'd bully the other adelitas if we made it official. But I've got to think about this deal a minute. No offense, but it's surprising how many bad habits a pretty girl can turn out to have, once you get to know her better."

She rose to her feet, stepping into the stream barefooted as she protested, "I do not lie. I do not steal. I never sleep with other men behind my soldado's back. I have no bad habits at all."

That wasn't quite true, he saw, as she reached down to pull her clothes off over her head and toss them on the bank, adding, "I have nothing at all to hide!"

He laughed and said, "That's for damned sure!" as he took in the inspiring sight of her breathtakingly desirable nude body, adding, with another fond chuckle, "I dunno, though. They say exhibitionism can become a bad habit, if you overdo it."

She didn't have a highly developed sense of humor, which seemed only fair when one considered how nicely everything else she had to offer was developed, so she pouted and said, "You are mocking me again, I think.

What can I do now for to convince you I am not a woman of concealed surprises?''

He stood up and proceeded to shuck his own duds and toss them on the grass as he said, ''Querida, if you revealed any more right now, I'd probably do something silly in my pants.''

She stared nervously as he stepped into the brook with her, naked and now fully aroused, and stammered, ''Oh, my, *you* were the one who was concealing a dangerous weapon, I fear! Forgive me, I may have spoken too soon. Perhaps we *had* better reconsider the idea after all!''

He took her firm warm body in his arms and lowered it, and his own, to the cool running water, pillowing her dark head on the grassy bank. He rolled atop her and spread her chunky brown thighs with his own as she asked, ''For why do you wish most of me under water, Captain Gringo?''

He said, ''For because I didn't bring along any axle grease, and, under the circumstances, you can call me Dick.''

Her big brown eyes opened wide in surprised dismay as he parted her now-cold and slippery love lips with the head of his wet erection and slid into her hot tunnel of love. The lubrication helped a lot. She'd had reason to be uneasy, with an opening as tight as that one. But he didn't seem to be hurting her, after all, as she spread her thighs wider, cupped his wet slippery buttocks in her palms, and gasped as she said, ''Oh, sí sí sí! I see what you *mean!*''

He kissed her to shut her up as they went deliciously crazy for a while. It felt kind of weird but wonderful as his rock-hard shaft felt flashes of hot and cold sliding in and out of her while their wet slippery bodies seemed to melt into one. He'd always enjoyed skinny-dipping. But this had doing it *alone* beat by a considerable margin.

For a dame who talked sort of dumb, Angelica sure knew how to kiss, too. The warmth of her darting tongue made another pleasant contrast to savor as he froze his nuts and warmed his shaft under the cool mountain water. He came. There was no reason to stop. So he didn't. Thanks

to the teasing, self-imposed celibacy he'd just put himself
through, he'd been hard up even before he'd guessed there
might be something as good as this within reach, and so,
as he reached her, she took it as a very generous compliment, and gasped as she said, "Oh, you are so simpático,
Deek! I just did, too, and . . . Ay, qué maravilloso, it is
happening *again,* and I feel so happy!"

That made two of them, with some reservations on his
part about just what he'd gotten himself into, aside from
the obvious. But she seemed a nice kid, he knew he'd have
wound up with one of the leftover adelitas anyway, and if
any of them screwed any *better,* he didn't want to know
about it. He had a lot of other activity facing him farther
up the trail, he knew, and a guy had to keep up his strength
in a war, too.

The next night on the trail went pleasantly indeed. The
next day was more complicated. As they continued south,
the trail kept rising higher and twisting more as it trended
sideways into ever-higher country. In places it humped
steeply, sagged through stretches of puddled mountain
runoff, or scared the shit out of everyone by running along
the edge of a sheer cliff for a while. At higher altitude
"rain forest" meant what it said, although at this time of
the year "fog forest" was more accurate. The constant
trades from the northeast seemed bent on condensing all
the moisture they had picked up crossing the Atlantic and
Caribbean on everything and everybody as they rose to
cross the spine bones of Central America. So everyone
marched cold and clammy in the fuzzy but dazzling
sunlight, surrounded by mossy trees and bushes that looked
as if elves lived under them. Captain Gringo tried to use
the cooler altitude to what advantage he could get out of
their discomfort by calling fewer trail breaks. The trail
breaks were getting complicated too.

Despite what he'd hoped without much hope, Angelica

was taking her new position as head adelita too seriously. A duller-witted man would not have noticed it. For, as many a born bitch had discovered in the past and would doubtless discover in the future, a strong-willed woman attached to a man in a position of power can abuse the shit out of others as long as she keeps *him* happy with her.

That part worked out nicely indeed for Captain Gringo. Angelica was such a good cook that her soldado could have wound up facing a weight problem had it not been for the considerable exercise the difficult trail and Angelica's delightful body put him through. In their bedroll at night, or anytime she could catch him alone during the day, Angelica couldn't seem to get enough sex, and, even better, she considered it her simple duty as his adelita to revive a semisated erection with amazing ingenuity for a bedmate too dull-witted to carry on an interesting conversation betweentimes.

Each time he prudently decided that this time a quickie would be enough, it turned into a protracted acrobatic orgy, and when he humorously accused her of attempting to drain him dry as a sucked lemon, she stopped sucking only long enough to say, demurely, that she wanted to make sure he was kept too sated even to wink at another woman.

But when Angelica wasn't doing nice things for her soldado, adelitas attached to lesser mortals approached her at their peril. Aside from natural jealousy, the little mestiza's lack of wit had hitherto made her the butt of female-army humor. So now that they were afraid to talk back to her, Angelica meant to pay them back with interest.

Her attempts at sarcasm fell short of cruel humor, since she had none, and hence simply translated as cruel pointless insults. On the rare occasions when an angry victim snapped back, Angelica fell back on warning them that she'd tell Captain Gringo on them, or, worse, that she already had, and that he'd said he'd do something awful if his own true love wasn't treated with the respect and admiration she was entitled to.

She never mentioned the other adelitas to him when they were alone, of course. For one thing, her mouth was often too full, and for another, she wasn't quite *that* dumb. So he got the name without the game, and might not have noticed anything at all had not so many of his people started looking at him as if he were an ogre, and a two-faced one at that, when he smiled pleasantly at them.

He asked her what was going on, of course. Sharing an after-sex cigar alone with her, he asked if she was having troubles with the other girls and, if so, why. Angelica simply fondled his genitals and snuggled her naked body closer to his as she suggested sweetly that naturally some of the others might be jealous of her, since he was so handsome.

It would have worked with most men. But Captain Gringo wasn't most men. He'd led troops before and could tell when they were just griping and when they really felt they had just cause to be thoroughly pissed off.

He thought, at first, that it might be the ever-present danger in irregular units of some Indian convincing his buddies that he'd make a better chief.

So, at a time when Angelica was cooking for him instead screwing him for the moment, he looked up Gaston for a council of war. It was an inconvenient moment for Gaston. The little Frenchman had finished his supper and was eating one of his adelitas for dessert as he laid the other. When Captain Gringo coughed politely outside the lean-to, Gaston looked up sheepishly, still moving his naked buttocks at the other end as both girls blushed and giggled, and said, "Feel free to join us, if you wish, my young and disgustingly virile. I seem to have bitten off more than a man my age can chew, non?"

Captain Gringo hunkered down, politely looking away, and he repressed a laugh as he said, "You seem to be chewing pretty good this evening. That's not my problem. We may have a pending mutiny on our hands. How do you feel about that?"

Gaston muttered, "Excuse me. I'm coming." Then

relaxed with a satisfied groan and, as the adelita under him kept moving and groaning pretty good herself, replied in a surprisingly even tone for anyone but Gaston, "As you see, these troops seem reasonably content with *my* leadership. I'm sure Dutch knows which side his bread is buttered on, and our native leaders already have more responsibility than they seem able to deal with. Naturally, there is always a frustrated military genius or two among the lower ranks. But naturally there are usually even more born tattletales, and I have heard no disturbing rumors, save for the complaints about your Angelica, of course."

"Oh? What's the gripe against her, Gaston?"

"Merde alors, how should I know? I am an officer, not an adelita. One assumes it is the usual jealousy. Her original solado was a barefoot peon who one hopes, for your sake, was devoid of loathsome diseases as well as brains. Her sudden rise up the ladder no doubt chagrined at least the extra adelitas we have on our hands. Since obviously, if you chose her above them, they could hardly claim to be as good a cook or a lay, non?"

"Oh, swell. That's probably it. That one black girl called Nina Brea has been shooting hurt looks at me that make me glad looks can't kill. How would you handle the situation, Gaston?"

Gaston began to move his rump politely as his adelita moaned and said she was coming, but kept his voice composed as he replied, "I am in no position, ridiculous as this position is, to help out that big black adelita they would not call the tar baby without reason. Why don't *you* try to comfort her, Dick? It would be more pratique, since you've more room in your bedroll than Dutch or I at the moment, hein?"

Captain Gringo laughed and said, "It's more crowded under the sheets with the one I've already got than one might think, just looking at her with her clothes on. Do you think Nina Brea is the main troublemaker among the adelitas?"

Gaston asked the one he was laying and she said she

didn't associate with niggers. The other adelita, sitting up as she fondled herself and shooting inviting smoke signals with her eyes, told Captain Gringo that Nina Brea was okay but probably felt rejected because of her complexion, since none of the other adelitas who'd seen her bathing naked doubted for a moment that she had the nicest body in camp.

He thanked all three of them for the information and headed back to his own lean-to as they went back to giving and taking head in an ingenious as well as no-doubt perverse reclining triangle.

He found Angelica waiting with soup on and clothes off. He hunkered down for a hasty meal as she kept begging him to hurry so they could have each other for dessert. He told her, "Hold my place for me until I get back. This is our last night camp before we reach the battle zone, and I want to make sure none of our pickets are doping off. This would be a dumb time to get caught with our pants down."

She told him to hurry back and take his pants down as he left without his hat or jacket, but naturally took along his shoulder-holstered .38.

He actually did make a tour of the extended camp, finding everything in order, nobody anxious to pick a fight with him and, when asked if anyone had any gripe, apparently as content with his leadership as any soldier is ever content with a chicken-shit, motherfucking, no-good son-of-a-bitching *officer!*

Sweeping around the camp, he found all the pickets where they'd been posted under the mossy trees. He made mental notes of who was posted where, then moved back into camp, where the handful of surplus adelitas were sharing a fire as well as their mutual misery, and snapped, "Nina Brea, I want to have a word with you alone."

As the not really tall but willowy black girl rose to her bare feet, eyes wide and wary in the firelight, another adelita murmured, "Uh-oh, *now* she's going to get it, poor thing!"

Captain Gringo wasn't supposed to hear that. So he

chose not to as he led the nervous black girl away from the fire and into the trees. He called out to the nearest picket, "Enrique, I'm conducting a military investigation and don't wish to be disturbed, understand?"

"I think so, Captain Gringo. Does that mean if anyone comes looking for you I am not to say where you went?"

"I just said that. Carry on, Soldado. You come with me, Nina Brea."

She did, but sobbed and asked if she could say her last prayers before she was shot. He didn't answer. Sometimes people spoke more freely when they were scared skinny.

He led her to a mossy fallen mahogany and told her to sit. She did so, like an obedient dog trying to avoid a whipping. He braced one boot heel on the same log, let her sweat as much as one could in the cool, damp night air as he lit a claro, then said, "You've been having trouble with my adelita. Tell me about it."

She sobbed and said, "As God is my witness, I did not *start* it, Captain Gringo! I did not even answer back, at first, but when a woman calls you a black slut no decent hombre would defile his body with, many times, one has trouble remembering her place."

"Keep talking."

"I did not hit her back. I swear I did not hit her back. I may be black, but I am not crazy. I only said bad words, a little, when she slapped my face and accused me of laughing at her behind her back."

"Have you been laughing at Angelica behind her back, Nina Brea?"

"Of course not! For what is there to laugh about? Does not she have it *all,* as the adelita of our commander?"

He repressed a dubious reply on that point to ask, "If you weren't laughing at her, why do you suppose she thought you were, Nina Brea?"

"Because she is, forgive me, not very bright, I fear. Ask any of the other mujers. They will tell you I do not lie, even though I am a woman of color."

He blew smoke out his nostrils like an annoyed bull and

said, "Let's cut out the color shit, Nina Brea. I don't care if you're black, brown, or sky blue. I'm simply trying to get to the bottom of this trouble you've been causing."

Nina Brea sobbed and answered, "You see? You *do* think I am the one who wishes for a fight! I know what you Yanquis think about black people. I am not completely uneducated. I can read. I know they have laws, up where you come from, against blancos y negros even sitting down beside one another!"

He sat down beside her on the log, instantly regretting it as his ass got wet, and said, "They have lots of funny laws in some parts of los Estados Unidos. That's why I had to leave so suddenly. I thought Latin Americans were more tolerant—though, come to think of it, I've been hit in the head more than once just for having light hair."

She shrugged and said, "It may be harder, down here, for to enforce ideas about color, since people come in so many. But your Angelica, for one, most certainly does not admire people whose ancestors may have had more African blood than hers. She has bedeviled me in particular more than any of the others, since she was able to boast of you coming in her all three ways."

He grimaced and said, "That was supposed to be our own little secret. Bueno, I'm beginning to get the picture. I can't say I *like* it much. So I'm open to suggestions, Nina Brea."

She shook her head and replied, "You would not like my suggestions."

But he insisted. So she said, "Shoot her. Then take another adelita who can be sweeter to the others."

"Oh, meaning you, Nina Brea?"

"Of course not. I know I am an ugly black woman in your eyes. But little Josefina has no soldado now, and she gets on well with everyone."

"Josefina's the little plump one with reddish hair, right?"

"Not all over. But she is most sweet, and before her soldado got killed, he boasted much of more than her cooking and ability to carry a pack."

"Wouldn't the other girls be jealous of *any* adelita I chose?"

"Sí, a little. But we don't hate Angelica so much for being head adelita as for because she is a stupid vicious bitch and . . . Oh, forgive me, I did not meant to go so *far*, Captain Gringo!"

He assured her, "I wanted you to tell me the truth. I've got enough on my plate without having to worry about hair-pulling contests among my own troops. I've got to stand up now. It's not because you're black. It's because this damp log is soaking through the seat of my pants and probably dyeing it green."

As he rose, she did, too, saying, "My poor black tail is even colder and wetter. These wet skirts feel most uncomfortable. If you do not mean to punish me, could we move back to the fire, por favor?"

He stared down at her dim form thoughtfully as he said, "I'm still working on it. It wouldn't be fair to punish you, if we assume you've told the truth."

"I was! I am! I swear!" she pleaded, moving closer in a woman's natural instinct to please a man when threatened. So he did what men usually do at such times, too, and her firm pear-shaped tits sure snuggled well against his shirt, even cold and damp. She asked timidly, "If I gave you a nice hot fuck, do you imagine you could find it in your heart for to forgive me?"

He laughed and said, "I imagine so. But this frigid mountain sex can become an uncomfortable habit, once the novelty wears off. Come on, I'll explain my solution along the way."

He did, and Nina Brea thought it was a swell idea that would solve lots of problems for both of them. But Angelica, reclined impatiently as well as nudely in the lean-to by the ruby light of the dying fire, didn't think much of Captain Gringo's plan as he and the black girl joined her.

She hissed, "Never! Never! You are mine, all *mine*,

Deek! And in any case I would *kill* myself before I would share any man with a vile black puta!''

Nina Brea dropped to her knees on the bedroll beside her and began to undress as she asked sweetly, ''Would you like me to cut your throat *for* you, little Indian, or do you intend to do it yourself?''

As Captain Gringo saw the body his invited guest was exposing to view in the ruby light, he forgot whatever misgivings he might still have, and Angelica soothed his conscience even further by snapping, ''Look at her! She's black as the tar she's named for, and I happen to know she sucks cock!''

He sat down between them and got to work on his own duds as he soothed, ''Come now, fair is fair, Angelica. You've been bragging all over camp about how good *you* are at that, too, you know.''

''It's not fair, it's not fair, it's not *fair!*'' Angelica wailed, throwing her chunky brown body against him as she pleaded, ''Haven't I been good to you, Querido? Haven't I filled your stomach well with Moors and Christians, as well as my stomach, with everything you wished for to put in it?''

He finished shucking, making sure the loaded .38 was empty as well as out of handy reach before answering, ''You've inspired me to greater heights, as a matter of fact. Okay, muchachas, who wants to go first?''

Angelica called both his mother and his father awful names and threw her tawny body prone at one end of the bedroll to beat and chew the already wilted bedding with angry fists and teeth. So he turned to Nina Brea with a raised eyebrow and a rising erection. She nodded eagerly and lay back sensuously atop the bedding, spreading her willowy black thighs in welcome.

So he found out why they called her the tar baby. Her sculpted ebony form was still cool to the touch from the chill night air. But her warm lush vagina welcomed his questing shaft in a clinging embrace that *could* remind a guy of sticking it in a tar barrel, he supposed, if anyone had ever been dumb enough to stick it in a tar barrel. He tried not to think how many others she'd treated so nicely, to get the nickname. The main trouble with love-'em-and-leave-'em sex was that everyone involved wanted it one-sided, with a partner who didn't screw so casually. But he decided to be a good sport about the black girl's dark past when she started to move that hot little tar pit in a way no certified virgin could have done on her wedding night with a prince.

They were going at it hot and heavy when Angelica looked up, her angry face facing their rollicking rumps, and sobbed as she said, "Oh, that's *mean!* Dammit, Nina Brea, I saw him *first!*"

The black girl put her back into it even better as she groaned and said, "Don't worry, little Indian. There's surely enough here for everybody! How on earth have you ever serviced this one without help? Doesn't he have a big one, though?"

Captain Gringo said, "Hey, are we trying to fuck or just show off, dammit?"

Nina Brea laughed lewdly and said, "Both. Pound me harder! As hard as you can! I'm really coming. No shit. You're *fantástico,* Deek!"

As he pounded her to glory, Angelica protested, "Call him Captain Gringo, you black bitch! Nobody but *me* has the right to be so familiar with him. Is that not right, Deek?"

He felt familiar as hell with the black, yeah, bitch, as he rammed it in as deep as it would go and ejaculated in her, with her own orgasmic spasms milking the full length of his shaft with hot pink velvet. As they went limp in each other's arms he sighed and murmured, "I don't care if she wants to call me shit-for-brains, right now. Whoever said variety was the spice of life sure knew what he was talking about."

Captain Gringo was a big man, and more than one woman in the past had complained of feeling crushed, afterward, so even though Nina Brea didn't ask him to

take a load off her tits he rolled off anyway, to lie
contentedly on his back between them while he considered
the mess he was probably in.

As Angelica hissed like the little engine that could and
forked a stockier as well as paler thigh across him, Nina
Brea grasped her intent before her intended victim did and
said, "Hey, I thought you were going to kill yourself,
Bitch."

Angelica spat, "I'll show you who the best lay in *this*
camp is, God damn your skinny black ass!" as, suiting
deeds to her words, she took the matter in hand and forced
it up inside herself, half-limp as it was, until it woke up in
such pleasant surroundings.

Captain Gringo was pleasantly surprised, too, as the
mestiza's chunky brown body proceeded to go up and
down atop him like a steam piston in heat. He thought it
would be impolite to twit her about her promise never to
share him with another woman. So he just let her, and
enjoyed it very much.

How could he have forgotten, so soon, what a great
little snatch old Angelica had? It felt nothing at all like
being in Nina Brea, bless them both. So the rest of the
evening went just swell, for him, and hopefully Angelica
wouldn't act so stuck up in the future.

The small Costa Rican garrison at Molina del Diablo
was under the command of a snotty second lieutenant who
doubtless would have acted snottier had not Captain Gringo been leading a regiment of pretty tough-looking guys
and even tougher-looking dames. The shavetail said to call
him Lieutenant Cabral and pointedly offered to produce his
commission as an officer for real. But Captain Gringo
politely told him to shove it back where it belonged, and
Cabral put it back in his pocket instead as the taller
American said he'd rather have a look around.

Leaving the irregulars camped under dripping pines with

everyone's but Angelica's morale much improved, Captain Gringo and Gaston tagged along with the snotty shavetail and didn't get to see anything more cheerful as he showed them how his defenses were set up.

The small regular unit was stationed in a sort of Alamo of one-story thick-walled buildings rapped around a flag-pole and courtyard. They were in position to dominate the north end of the spidery steel bridge arching out across a canyon that had to be, as its name would indicate, the handiwork of the devil. Looking down over the guardrail of the bridge afforded a gut-wrenching view of the white waters milling like a devil's mill indeed a quarter mile or so straight down. They could see why Costa Rica didn't want to have to build this bridge *twice*. How they'd done so the first time was seasickening to think about.

On the far side of the chasm the same trail they'd followed this far left the plank decking of the bridge to knife directly into a wall of tall timber. The cover came right to the rim of the canyon in places. So Captain Gringo asked Cabral, "Is this big crack in Mother Earth's ass the border? I thought it was a few miles south."

Cabral frowned and said, "It is. At least fifty kilometers, depending on whose map one reads. Why?"

"If Costa Rica owns all that cover on the far side, it ought to come down. Be easy enough to snake the logs over the rim and let the water down below deal with 'em. I'd have my boys clear a field of fire at least past rifle range and then, if there was still time, I'd have 'em clear back further."

Cabral sniffed and said, "They are not your boys. They are *mine*. And I have taken my *own* precautions here. I assure you nobody is about to cross this bridge while *I* have anything to say about it."

Gaston spat over the side experimentally and asked, "Eh bien, how much are you liable to have to *say* about it, once a sniper round from those too-close trees takes you in your adorable little head, Lieutenant? I have not won a sharpshooter's badge on the rifle range for some time now.

But one imagines a competent, or lucky, marksman could break the window glass of your jolly little fortress from any number of those très pushy trees under discussion, non?"

Cabral shrugged and said, "Remind me to keep my shutters closed at night. I have no authority to cut timber on that privately owned land across the canyon, in any case."

Captain Gringo asked, "Who owns it, the mountain elves?" and Cabral replied, without a trace of humor, "I believe some European timber syndicate is holding all that pine in reserve. There is nobody living among it, at the moment."

Captain Gringo said, "You mean you *hope*. Okay, who is living beyond on the far side—on *our* side, I mean?"

"Nobody important. Just a few scattered Indian settlements north of the official border through uninhabited rain forest for the most part. Naturally those nominal Costa Ricans fleeing a serious invasion should give us plenty of warning, here, as they stream across the only crossing for many kilometers in any direction."

"Warning to do what?" asked Captain Gringo, with a thoughtful glance back at the little undermanned outpost.

Cabral replied, "For to blow this bridge, of course. If there is no bridge across Molina del Diablo, I have little else to worry about, no?"

Gaston snorted in disgust and said, "Mais non, only your commission. Hasn't anyone told you the whole point of our expedition is to *save* this ugly but no doubt très expensive span, Lieutenant?"

Cabral tried, and failed, to hide a sneer as he replied, "It is not *our* expedition. It is *your* expedition. My orders are simply that should you not be able to discourage a full-fledged invasion in this sector, I am to do my best. And the best I can possibly do with a mere handful of troops and no heavy weapons is a full demolition of this only crossing."

Captain Gringo signaled Gaston not to argue the point

further. Then he asked the shavetail, "Is this bridge wired for sound right now?"

Cabral nodded and replied, "Sí. We are in no danger, I assure you. The charges are safe sixty-percent-nitro Du Pont dynamite, fused with new electric caps."

"Oh boy! Who's holding the other end of the wire?"

"Nobody. The magneto box is in my office under lock and key. Not yet connected to the fuse wires, of course. They, at the moment, are wrapped around one leg of my desk, should the time arise to blow this bridge. Until then, I don't see how any accidents could happen."

Captain Gringo could, given a chicken-shit officer who could walk out on this span almost any old time. But he didn't mention that. He just said, "Okay, make sure you don't blow this fucking bridge up behind us. What do you think, Gaston? Two companies across with one left here in reserve?"

Gaston shrugged and replied, in English, "That is the way it is usually done. Mais somehow I would feel safer if we left Dutch, *two* companies of riflemen and of course all the adelitas here to await our safe return across this adorable erection, hein?"

The trouble with switching languages was that almost anyone spoke English when you didn't want him to. Cabral scowled and asked, in the same language, "Do you suggest my men and me are not to be trusted?"

Captain Gringo laughed easily and said, "Take it easy, Lieutenant, old Gaston wouldn't trust his mother with his ass, and you don't look anything like her."

"Was that a remark regarding my manhood, Yanqui?"

"No. I'm sure you stand up when you piss. It's your *nerves* we're worried about. Let's go back to the others."

Captain Gringo and Gaston did. Cabral peeled off to duck back into his command post as the soldiers of fortune passed it on their way to camp.

Dutch Lansford agreed that it might be a good idea to keep as many eyes on the nervous shavetail as possible while they figured out the situation. So Gaston proceeded to gather what was more a heavy combat patrol of men picked from various companies than a company, as Captain Gringo, playing a sudden hunch, said he'd meet 'em at the bridge when they were ready to move out.

The Costa Rican either guarding the entrance to the headquarters building or reading a dirty magazine, depending on how his corporal of the guard chose to view it, said that, sí, the lieutenant was in his office and offered to go get him. Captain Gringo said, "I wouldn't want to disturb your rest, Soldado. I can find him. Tell me something. How long have you muchachos served under Cabral, anyway?"

The uniformed private looked blank. Then he said, "Let me see, at least a week now. He came in as a replacement for Lieutenant Robles, who deserted, sí, about a week ago."

Captain Gringo thanked him and stepped over his boots to go on in, moving on the balls of his feet as he made his way down the corridor to a closed door marked OFICIO DEL COMANDANTE as he got out his double-action .38.

He gently tried the knob with his free hand. It didn't turn. He hadn't expected it to. So he stepped back and kicked the door in.

Lieutenant Cabral leaped up from behind his desk like a flushed duck as Captain Gringo barged in, gun in hand, and demanded, "What is the meaning of this, Señor!"

Captain Gringo kicked the ruined door shut behind him with a boot heel and replied, "Better to be safe than sorry. Step out from behind that desk and drop your pants."

"Are you insane? Why on earth would I wish for to do that?"

"Because I'll kill you if you don't," Captain Gringo said flatly.

But Cabral must not have wanted to drop his pants, because he went for his sidearm instead. So Captain Gringo shot him, twice, and as the body still drummed one heel like a dying sidewinder on the floor, he stepped around and over it to see what else the cocksucker had been trying to hide from him.

The magneto box was under the keyhole of the office desk, fully wired with its plunger ready to detonate everything connected to the other ends. So Captain Gringo swore and dropped to one knee to disconnect the wires with one savage yank. As he straightened up, the door flew open again and the same sentry he'd spoken to before gasped and said, "I warn you, Captain Gringo, I am covering you!"

The American said, "No, you're not. You're holding that rifle at port and I'm pointing this gun more logically. If you want to do something useful, go get your sergeant of the guard and tell him *he's* in command now. What are you waiting for, soldado, a kiss good-bye? *Move!*"

The guard ran off, muttering something under his breath about crazy officers in general and gringo ones in particular. So the next ones who turned up were Gaston and Dutch.

Gaston said, "We heard shots, Dick. Is anything wrong here?" Then he spotted the body and sighed. "Oui, I thought we heard a .38."

Captain Gringo said, "The trouble was supposed to catch up with us out in the middle of that bridge. I just jumped the gun with a lucky hunch. Hold it. We have company dropping in on us."

The burly sergeant of the guard and as many Costa Rican troopers as could fit in the doorway with him were all pointing wary rifles Captain Gringo's way. So he asked, "What took you guys so long? We've got a sort of tricky situation here."

The sergeant frowned down at the body and replied, "Es verdad, Yanqui! I shall ask you one time for why you just shot our commandante, and it had better be good!"

Captain Gringo said, "I think it is. In the first place, I didn't shoot your Costa Rican lieutenant. I shot a ringer sent to take his place. Did you jerk-offs really *buy* the story of a commissioned officer *deserting* a post that wasn't even under attack, for God's sake?''

The sergeant looked uncertain and replied, ''It did seem a little odd. But who were *we* to question what any officer might or might not do?''

''That's what they were counting on. They waylaid your original officer some way, probably made him take off his uniform before they murdered him, then sent this asshole to take his place. Fortunately, he was a lousy actor as well as a sneak. No second lieutenant, ever, acts that snotty to anyone who might possibly outrank him.''

''In God's truth, he was not very popular, Captain Gringo, but can you prove any of your suspicions? I mean no disrespect, but if one was allowed to shoot second lieutenants just for being assholes, there would not be many left before long, no?''

Captain Gringo laughed and said, ''Gaston how's about showing them the facts of life while I keep the odds polite with this pisoliver?''

Gaston nodded, dropped to one knee, and pulled down the corpse's pants and underdrawers with a jerk that might have made Cabral wince, had he been able to.

Everyone but Gaston and Captain Gringo gasped. The sergeant asked, ''What could have happened to the lieutenant's balls, for God's sake?''

Captain Gringo said, ''He let them castrate him years ago, and he probably thought it *was* for God's sake, the poor chump. He's a member of a fanatic order of military monks calling themselves Los Jurados. They train military. So they know how to act military when they have to, and this one had to. His mission was to stop us, and he almost did. We'll find out *why* on the lonesome side of the bridge, I hope, now that he can't blow it up with us on it!''

They all seemed impressed. Even Gaston asked, as he straightened up, ''*How,* Dick? I, of course, had him down as a species of idiot. But since I can't see through men's pants, even if I wished to do such a disgusting thing, and . . .''

Captain Gringo cut in to explain, "I wasn't sure. His soldier act just rubbed an old soldier wrong. All shavetails look like sissies to me at this late date. So even though he carried it beyond the call of duty, I gave him the chance to prove he was all man, and, had I been wrong, I'd have felt dumb as hell. But he didn't. So I don't."

Dutch Lansford sighed and said, "When you told me these Jurados you brushed with before were fanatics, you didn't fib much. But doesn't all this mean Los Jurados must know we're coming?"

"If they weren't worried about us dropping in on them, they wouldn't have tried to *stop* us. Old Pablo's deathbed confession's starting to smell a bit fishy, too. But that's ancient history. So's *this*. Sergeant! Are you paying any attention to this conversation?"

"Sí, with more interest than you might imagine, Captain Gringo!"

"Bueno. Attention to orders. Captain Lansford here will be in command of this bridge crossing until the rest of us get back. You'll do as he says, just as he says, and someday you'll get to tell your grandchildren how you saved your country. You fuck up, and they'll never *know* their poor old grandfather. Any questions?"

"Sí. My men and me are regulars, and, meaning no disrespect, the other captain, here, is not even Costa Rican, let alone a commissioned Costa Rican officer."

"You wanna tell him, Dutch? Or should I?"

Dutch grinned and faced the regular sergeant as he said soothingly, "I think the sergeant understands that when a guy backed with four times the guns yells 'froggy,' it's a good idea to jump. Ain't that right, Sarge?"

"Oh, well, when you put it that way, who are we to argue? It is up to the government to sort the paperwork out in any case, no?"

Dutch turned back to Captain Gringo and said, "You see, we're going to get along just fine together here, Dick."

Captain Gringo said, "I sure hope so. I'm not looking

to getting back across that canyon the hard way. I hardly ever fly, and it's sure as hell too wide for *Puss in Boots* to *jump!*''

If they didn't make it, Dutch was going to need more firepower than they could leave him to get the others out alive. But Captain Gringo and Gaston took the extra machine gun, two hundred riflemen, and enough ammo to leave Dutch feeling wistful. Once across the bridge, they put a five-man diamond out on point, with additional scouts out on either flank whether they enjoyed it under the dripping trees or not. Captain Gringo told everybody to bear on the twisting trail until further notice because, even following the trail, he wasn't sure just where the hell he was leading them.

The map didn't say just where between here and the border the reported scattered villages might be, and, in truth, the border itself was punctuated with question marks on the map. But the distant central government wouldn't have built the bridge and a fairly decent trail if it didn't lead *somewhere*, right?

He had to think about that when, about a mile and a half down the trail they were following, *another* cut across it at a right angle. He said, ''What the fuck . . . ?'' and got out his map again as he stood with Gaston in the middle of the crossroads.

He swore some more when he saw, as he'd already been almost certain, that neither the crossroads nor anything crossing the main drag in this neck of the woods was on the damned map.

It was far from clear which was the most important trail now, too. The one they'd been following looked more impressive on the map than in real life, littered with pine cones and too narrow for two-wheeled vehicles to pass each other without scraping hubs on trees as well as each other. The mysterious cross trail was a wider wagon trace that looked more traveled. As Captain Gringo stared at the uninhabited pine plantation all around, he couldn't help wondering who the hell was traveling where in this map sector. He told Gaston, "The only answer I can come up with is a logging road someone didn't see fit to tell the guys who drew this map about. Lemme see, map's dated 1878. Yeah, that could explain it."

Gaston said, "Oui, the cartographers may have just traced over an even older map when they drew that one nearly twenty years ago. But I doubt this mysterious passage through the forest primeval is a logging trail, Dick. When one logs, one leaves stumps, non? Regardez, we are not only lost, we are lost in virgin forest! Even in the tropics it takes *some* time to grow tall timber, and some of those trees are taller than *you* are!"

"Yeah, nobody's laid an ax to anything around here since Columbus took that wrong turn to India, save for clearing this wagon trace. They told us back at Molina del Diablo that some syndicate was holding everything around here in reserve, too. Okay, screw *why* they built this new road. Let's *follow* the little basser and see what happens."

As he whistled in his scouts to give them new bearings, Gaston asked, "Is this trip really necesario, Dick? What's wrong with the original trail we've *been* following? At least it's on the map, so we can't get lost, hein?"

"It'll still be on the map when we find out where *this* one goes. Meanwhile, some sore losers have been busting a gut trying to prevent us from doing . . . whatever the hell we're doing, and *they* could have old survey maps too, you know."

"Bless you, my child. On sober reconsideration, this wagon trace does seem a much pleasanter thoroughfare after all!"

Nobody else wanted to argue. So once they had the outfit re-formed, they followed the mysterious trace, and as they did so, it soon became evident that it followed a contour line leading neither up nor down but winding some to maintain its level grade more or less in line with the impassable canyon to the north. Gaston spotted a horse apple along the edge of the trail and observed, "Regardez, at least one rider passed this way no more than a few days ago. How come we get to walk so much, Dick?"

"Remind me to give our point man hell for not reporting that, next time we take a break. We're walking because I'm not as worried about cavalry as I am legged-up Colombian infantry, up here among these wooded hills. It's rough country to push horses through, off the trails."

"Merde alors!" Gaston snorted. "He accuses me of talking too much and he gives an old campaigner, such as I, lectures on basic tactics?"

Captain Gringo told him to shut up, raised a hand to halt their column, and sniffed again suspiciously. Gaston said, "Oui, I smell it, too. Do not people stink, all too soon, after what might otherwise be a dignified end?"

The getaway man of their forward diamond came running back along the wagon trace to call out, "Dead hombres! Many dead hombres! Corporal Valdez said you might wish for to know!"

"Corporal Valdez just saved his invisible stripes. What's the story up ahead?"

The scout made the sign of the cross and replied, "In God's truth, we didn't know what to make of it, Captain Gringo. We simply came upon a cadaver lying by the trail. Then, when we fanned out for to scout the situation, we found more. Many more. They are all about in the woods, missing their boots, weapons, and in some cases they've been stripped to their underwear."

"Underwear? Hm, peones don't get to wear much underwear. Any sign of the trouble they obviously ran into, ah, Sanchez?"

"No, Captain Gringo. They just lie there, dead. About three or four days, from the flies and smell. Maybe more. Flesh takes longer to rot up here in the cooler highlands, and the vultures do not seem to have noticed them under the dense trees."

Captain Gringo nodded and moved on, asking the scout

where the point man and the other three were, ahead. Sanchez said they'd dug in to await further orders and added, "Pepe wished for to scout ahead. But Corporal Valdez said that is not the way it is done. Was he right, Captain Gringo?"

"He may have just made sergeant. Scouts are not supposed to fight if they don't have to, and, if and when they make contact with the enemy, they're not supposed to let the enemy know they're around. So he did right indeed. How far do we have to go, Sanchez? Never mind, I can hear the flies now."

They found the first body before they found their point. The corpse lay face down, so bloated it had split the seams of its dark blue pants. Captain Gringo asked Gaston if that shade of blue looked familiar, and the little Frenchman said, "Oui, please don't ask me to pull *that* one's pants down. I'll take your word he used to be a Jurado."

Sanchez gasped and said, "Madre de Dios! Are all these dead hombres those muy loco fighting monks you warned us about, Captain Gringo?"

"Don't know. Haven't seen 'em all yet. Where the hell's Valdez?"

The point man provided his own answer by stepping out into view on the wagon trace, calling out as he approached, "I am sorry, Captain Gringo. I make no excuses for myself. You let me pick my patrol and I picked that estupido Pepe. But he did not manage for to get himself killed after all."

"Valdez, will you back up and start at the damned beginning? I know Pepe's an eager kid. The question is what did he *do,* not why."

"He moved on ahead, Captain Gringo. But I don't think anyone at that estancia saw him, and at least he had sense enough to report back when he could advance no further without crossing open ground."

Captain Gringo swore, shook his head, and said, "There you go again. What estancia? How far? How much open ground? You're supposed to start a report at the *beginning*, you ass-backwards hablador!''

"I know. Forgive me. I am excited. The forest ends just ahead. Beyond lies a cleared stretch of corn milpas with the farmhouse and outbuildings maybe four hundred meters from the tree line and . . ."

"Let's have a look, then," Captain Gringo cut in, pressing forward. As they did so, they saw other dead Jurados, lots of other dead Jurados, rotting all around them under the pines. Gaston observed, "Good shooting, non?" and the tall American said, "Impossible shooting, from that farmhouse, unless Valdez counts lousy."

"Oui, with the tree line at a range calling for some skill, and this species of fly fodder well inside the trees, one would assume our sharpshooting farmers would have missed at least a *few* of them."

Valdez led them to where the overeager Pepe and another scout were peeking over a fallen log like gnomes at a cluster of tile-roofed, buff-colored stucco buildings out in the middle of an ominous expanse of cut corn stubble. Pepe glanced up and said, eagerly of course, "Nothing seems to be moving at any of the windows and there are no horses in the corrals, Captain Gringo!"

Captain Gringo had been young and eager once, too, so he said, "If you ever break away from your patrol leader again to go in business for yourself, make sure you just keep going. The next time it happens, I'll shoot you for desertion. Do we understand each other, Soldado?"

"Sí, Captain Gringo. It won't happen again."

Captain Gringo didn't answer, since the matter was closed. But as he hunkered down behind the log with them and Gaston, he asked the Frenchman, "You see any dead horses around here?"

Gaston shook his head and said, "That may have been what these Jurados were after when they attacked, hein? Obviously they failed to get what they were after. So the farmers who beat them off must have ridden off with their horses, non?"

Captain Gringo thought before he shrugged and said, "That works as good as anything I can come up with. Cover me. I'm going in."

As he rose, Gaston asked, "Dick, do you think that's wise? Someone over there behind those trés mysterious walls did some très fancy shooting not too long ago!"

"I make it more like four or five days ago, and it wasn't fancy shooting. It was just plain impossible. We can't just stay here *staring* at the damned place if we're ever going to move on. You, Pepe, you're so fucking eager. Run back and tell Rojas and Montoya to get that machine gun over here on the double."

Then, as Pepe ran back through the pines, Captain Gringo stepped out of them into the open, removing his hat to wave it as a substitute truce flag he sure hoped someone might respect.

Behind him, Gaston called out, "Wait, you species of suicidal maniac! At least let me cover you with the Maxim as you forge on across that stupid stubble!"

Captain Gringo didn't answer or look back. It wouldn't matter if the machine gun was set up or not if anybody spotted him out here in the open. It wouldn't matter, to him, whether Gaston avenged him or not. Though there was some small satisfaction in knowing that the sometimes-moody little Frenchman surely would. Somebody had to risk it, if they meant to go on, and going on was the whole point in the deadly trade of war. He was too good a warrior to order another to do such a goddamned stupid thing.

He spotted another dead Jurado, off to his far right, and kept walking as he muttered, "What were *you* doing out here all alone, little girl? Oh, right, you bought it in the first advance. Your buddies ran back to the tree line, and, shit, after that it just won't work, will it?"

He spotted movement at the window near the front door of the main house and waved again as he made for it. Nobody waved back. He spotted yet another fallen attacker, off to his far left, fertilizing next season's crop pretty good, since the vultures *had* found him and he was oozing nicely into the soil indeed.

As Captain Gringo got within hearing range of the door, it opened a crack and a double-barreled shotgun peered out at him to say, in a surprisingly feminine tone, "Far enough, Señor! Who are you and for why are you on our land?"

He called back, "It's all right. I'm on *your* side, Señora. Your own government sent us down this way to see if you needed just the kind of help you obviously needed not long ago! What happened to your horses and, no offense, your menfolk here?"

"I am alone here now. The ladrónes took our horses, of course."

"And your menfolk?"

There was a long sad pause, followed by, "Out back. I buried them as well as I could, after dark, after the ladrónes rode off. You may come a little closer, if you keep your hands courteous, Señor. I can see you do not look like those with either attacking band. But I warn you, I am a good shot!"

He moved on in, observing, "You sure must be, Señora, or is it Señorita?"

The door opened, revealing the armed figure of an otherwise not bad brunette who answered soberly, "I am the Widow Herrera, now. It has been almost a week since they killed my husband. Come in. I am sorry if you find the place a mess. But I was not expecting company today."

He stepped inside the cooler shade as the young widow made room for him but kept the shotgun in one slim fist, albeit now pointed more politely.

As his eyes adjusted to the light, he gazed around at the bullet-pocked walls and furniture piled at the windows and whistled softly before he said, "You're earlier visitors sure were rude, Señora! But suppose you tell me how *you* came out of whatever happened alive. It sure must not have been too easy!"

The widow sighed and said, "It wasn't. Starting from the beginning. We were hit about a week ago, I have lost track of the days, by men in strange blue uniforms. They simply marched out of the trees and proceeded to shoot at us. But, fortunately, we had just cut the last of the corn stalks and everyone was close enough to the buildings for to get inside, even though two of our peones died that night of their wounds."

"Then your husband and his boys drove them back to the tree line, eh?"

"I helped. I told you I was a good shot. For two, three, maybe more days and nights they besieged us. First my poor Carlos, then the other men were picked off, one by one. It was very sad, Señor."

"I'll bet it was. But they sure did a job on the guys over there shooting at you from those trees! Must be over a hundred bodies under the pines now. I can see you had better cover, here, but . . ."

"I don't know if we hit *any* of them, once they made it back to the tree line," the widow cut in with a fatalistic shrug, adding, "In the end we were saved by the *second* gang. It must have surprised the first gang, too, when the first thing anyone on either side knew, this loco gun was hammering like a woodpecker, papapapapapapa!"

He blinked and asked, "Do you mean the second gang had a *machine* gun, Señora?"

"I do not know what kind of a machine it was. It most certainly made a lot of noise. The second gang of course fired rifles as well. A lot of rifles, from the sound of it all!"

He nodded and said, "Yeah, old Pablo always was a noisy guy. I'm starting to put it together now. The leader of the second gang was just a ladrón with a grudge against Los Jurados, after all."

The widow looked puzzled and asked, "What are Los Jurados? I mean, I know jurados are the people who decide if one is innocent or guilty of a crime, but those men in blue looked like some sort of *soldados* to me, Señor."

"Maybe they thought they were both. Let's not lose the thread, por favor. What happened after the second gang wiped out the first gang?"

"I hid, up the chimney, hoping this warm weather would last, in the name of God. So they did not find me when they barged in for to plunder the house of valuables, such as we had. From the sounds I heard, praying very quietly in the sooty shaft, they did not stay long. They simply told coarse jokes, helped themselves to whatever they wished, then left—with our livestock, of course."

He nodded understandingly. It was a familiar tale and he didn't imagine she wanted to hear that her beef, pork, and chickens were long gone. But he said, "Your horses are alive and well in San Mateo, Señora. We left them in the care of the padre there."

The shotgun muzzle flinched. So he quickly added, "Wait! I know this because my guerrilla wiped out the second bunch up there and . . . Hold it. I'd better back up and start at the beginning, too. It sounds confusing to *me*, and *I* know what *happened*, now!"

The Widow Herrera was afraid to stay alone at the shot-up estancia, which seemed reasonable, didn't want to head for the bridge crossing all alone, which seemed reasonable, and wanted to go on with Captain Gringo's combat patrol, which didn't, but what was left?

Gaston argued in favor of taking the sole survivor of the wild siege along, pointing out, "We could use a guide who knows this country, and, as you probably saw first, dammit, she's not bad-looking."

Captain Gringo grimaced and said, "She's okay, if you like 'em sort of tall and skinny. But down, Boy. The poor dame just lost the man she started out with, for chrissake."

"Eh bien, but who's to say it was a happy marriage? I can't help noticing she was wearing a floral print, not black, when you waved us in back there."

Captain Gringo swore and added, "Asshole, the poor dame can't wear widow's weeds till she has a chance to get to a dress shop, for God's sake. She's probably wearing the only decent dress she has. She told me she ruined one scrooching up the chimney and probably staining it with more than soot. So keep your pecker in your pants, you old fart. I *mean* it."

Gaston protested that he only comforted widows when requested politely, and then shut up, just in time, as the widow they were talking about moved up the marching column to fall in with them, walking pretty well, for a woman, in a stout pair of boots. Captain Gringo had been worried about that and started to ask if they were her late husband's boots. But he decided it wouldn't be delicate. Instead, he asked if she had any idea where the trail they were following led.

She said, "Sí, to the next bridge crossing to the east and perhaps beyond. I have never ridden further east. There is another north–south road, an old stage road, joining this wagon trace at the old crossing."

Captain Gringo frowned and said, "Wait a minute! The map says there's not supposed to *be* another bridge across that damned canyon to our north!"

The widow shrugged and said, "There *isn't,* now. I just told you it was the *old* crossing. A hanging rope bridge, built by the Indians long ago, and even when new, it was a most treacherous way for to get across. I suppose when the government built the new bridge at Molina del Diablo the lazy Indians saw no further reason to keep the old rope bridge in repair. This new trail, of course, was laid out for to lead travelers from the old route to the new one, no?"

"Makes sense. I'd sure hate to follow the old stage road all the way up here only to find my path barred by one big hole in the ground. How far is this other crossing we're talking about, Señora?"

"Perhaps a full day's march, as your hombres are marching. There is nothing between here and there but the trees you see all about us. If you insist on going on, we shall have to camp in the woods tonight, I fear.''

He shrugged and said, ''I insist on all sorts of things. It was your idea to come along, Señora. If your fears include any of my men getting forward with you, forget it. We'll manage the spare bedding from their light packs, somehow, and these muchachos are the cream of our crop. They won't get fresh or do anything else we don't order them to.''

''I hope you are right. I am at your mercy, alone and unarmed.''

''I noticed you left that shotgun behind, Señora. How come? Too heavy?''

''Too empty,'' she replied with a sad little smile.

He laughed and said, ''You sure bluff good, Señora! By the way, do we have to keep calling you Señora? This is Gaston, and I'm called Dick, by my friends.''

The young widow looked uncertain, then said, ''I am called Celia, by *my* friends. Or I was, when I still had any. Forgive me, I seem to have something in my eye.''

Captain Gringo put a comforting hand on her shoulder. She flinched away like a spooked fawn. So he added quickly, ''Nobody wants to be *that* friendly, Celia. I told you we knew how to behave in mixed company. So why don't you just relax, eh?''

''You call the pace you set relaxing?'' She sighed, adding, ''You all walk so fast, and these men's boots are so big on my poor feet!'' Then, before he could say it, she added, ''I know, I know, you told me to stay in the house and you'd pick me up on the way back. But I just *couldn't*, Deek!''

He glanced up at the sun, raised his hand to call a halt, and said, ''Trail break.'' Then he looked around for his nearest native noncom, found one, and called out, ''Robles, drop anything you have to drop in the woods and get back to me on the double with your platoon.''

Then he led the limping widow over to the shady grass beside the trail and sat her down, remaining on his feet with Gaston as he told her softly, "I know this may not sound delicate, Celia. But if you'd like to scamper off and pick mushrooms or something . . ."

Celia sighed and said, "I do not have to relieve myself, Deek. I just need for to rest my feet a little."

He observed that she needed to rest them a lot as he hunkered down beside her and lit a claro. Gaston flopped face down in the grass and told them to wake him up when it was time to get up again.

Captain Gringo and the young widow sat awhile, trying to ignore the inevitable sexual tension between any attractive adults wearing skirts or pants respectively until, a million years later, Sergeant Robles joined them to report that his platoon was ready for whatever Captain Gringo had in mind.

Captain Gringo said, "Bueno. What I have in mind is for you to escort Señora Herrera here back to the bridge crossing at Molina del Diablo. Carry her if you have to, but get back there before dark."

"I understand, Captain Gringo. Do you wish for us to try to catch up with you again?"

"I wish you could. But don't try it. Your thirty rifles will be of more use to Captain Lansford's garrison than floundering around out here lost in the woods. I don't know where we'll be going from here, exactly, and I'm not about to leave a blazed trail behind me on this side of that damned canyon!"

He glanced at Celia and added, "They're ready when you are, Celia. I know you're tired. But if you don't start poco tiempo you'll never make Molina del Diablo this side of sunset."

He got to his feet and put out a hand to help her to hers without waiting for a reply. So she had little choice but to get back up with a sigh and go with God and Sergeant Robles.

As soon as they were out of earshot, Gaston muttered, still face down in the grass, "You know, of course, you just pissed away a third of our force?"

Captain Gringo shrugged and asked, "What was I supposed to do, shoot her? I'd have sent her back with more, if we could have spared 'em. But thirty rifles ought to get a pretty girl safely back a few miles. She sure as shit wasn't about to march on much farther with *us*. If you mean to take a piss, you'd better do so, pronto. As soon as they're out of sight, we're pushing on."

"Merde alors, an old soldier like me does not have to stop for piss call. Not walking at the head of the column, at any rate."

Captain Gringo laughed, forcing himself to rest while he could, by flopping down beside Gaston in the grass, saying, "I've always said I admired a man who could think on his feet." Then he frowned, sat up, and added, "Speaking of thinking on one's feet, I forgot to ask that dame something, but, shit, it's probably not worth chasing her."

"What did she leave out, since you didn't seem interested in her time of the month?"

"That farm back there. What was it *doing* there?"

"Merde alors, growing corn, of course," Gaston began. Then he nodded and said, "Ah, oui, off the beaten track and all that. Smugglers, perhaps?"

Captain Gringo thought before he shrugged and said, "No. Makes more sense as a trail break selling fodder for horses, mules, and such. She said guys using the older trail a day to the east have to detour along this one now to reach the new bridge crossing."

He took out the map again, studied it, and asked, "Gaston, have you ever had the feeling some lying cocksucker was feeding you a line of shit?"

"Many many times. How did you know that lady sucked cock? Some of these unsophisticated Hispanic country folk can be tediously conservative about such matters."

"I didn't catch *her* in a lie. I just caught *them* in a lie."

"Oh? Which them are we discussing, Dick?"

"I'm not sure. But look, this fucking map doesn't show

this trail we're on, the apparently well-traveled stage route to the east, or the other bridge crossing Celia said they met at!''

"Perhaps she was confused, in her present state?"

"She could be confused or crazy as a bedbug. The fact remains this crazy map doesn't show a stage route and detour traveled well enough to rate at least one farm making a living peddling corn to *some* damned body! They had a good quarter section cleared back there. Saying they use the old Hispanic three-field system, that still leaves one hell of a lot of corn and probably produce to sell travelers by the side of a road that ain't suppose to *be* here!''

Gaston rolled over and sat up, asking, "What do you suggest, that we have as usual been crossed double? By whom, Dick? Would it make any sense for the most plotting of plotters to send us in quest of the goose savage? If the Costa Rican government did not want us to find anything down this way, would not it have been much easier not to send us at all?''

Captain Gringo didn't answer. So Gaston continued, "I have, as you may have surmised, been crossed double by experts in my time. But I must say I'd be most surprised by anyone stupid enough to arm and outfit such a force at great expense, only to send them off to simply get lost, non?''

Captain Gringo said, "The legit government does want its borders secured in this area. We were recruited by them, paid front money by them, and armed by them to do exactly the job they told us they wanted us to do. After that, it gets murky. Someone we've met in our travels is a sneak who wants this mission to fail. So someone *switched maps* on us. I was *wondering* why it was almost old enough to vote.''

"Sacre God damn! Are you suggesting someone played the pickpocket in reverse somewhere between here and San José, Dick?''

"No. I'm too fucking smart. But if someone simply

switched the map the military was supposed to issue us, back at GHQ, who'd be likely to notice? When one guy hands another guy a folded map, stamped with the proper survey numbers, is he liable to unfold it to make sure it's not a map of Greece?''

"Eh bien, my dear Uncle Claude back in Paris, the one who tried to convince me sodomy was good for a young boy's bowels, also said the best confidence games are the simple ones, hein? I am beginning to see the light. We've been sent because orders came down from high places to send us. We were sent after the goose savage because some most ambitious officer or group of officers further down the pole of totems grows fatigued with waiting for advancement and would like to see the military expanded, as it no doubt would be, in the face of an invasion we failed to stop the cheap way. Who do you think, Colonel Vegas?''

"Could be. Wouldn't have been smart of Vegas to recruit guys as good as us, though. San José's full of knockaround guys who could probably get just as lost with an up-to-date map. I'm betting on some junior officer or officers, probably pissed because they sent us instead of giving him or them a spanking-new regiment of regulars.''

Gaston nodded and said, ''That makes more sense. Has it occurred to you, yet, where that leaves *us*, Dick? We have our front money. If we simply go back and report we were given nothing to work with, we could spare our adorable selves a lot of fatigue, if not dying, non?''

''Non. Some motherfucker set us up to blow it, and I'm just not going to give him the *satisfaction!* Let's go. We've spent enough time on our butts just talking about it. I want to find out what the hell is going on, and we sure as shit can't find out sitting here!''

Neither the moon nor Captain Gringo allowed a full bivouac that night. As an experienced campaigner in

Apache country, their leader let them break for grub at
sunset and told them to quit their bitching when they had
to down their tortillas and jerked beef cold. They got time
to have a smoke or take a shit, not both, and then the big
fat tropic moon was up and painting the wagon trace
silver, so they hit it.

He gave them a ten-minute trail break once an hour on
the hour and made them make up the lost time by marching
faster than most of them had ever walked in their lives
before meeting up with him and Gaston. Captain Gringo
had long since learned that the seeming laziness of the
tropical peon was a hasty as well as unfair assumption. He
knew that because of the sultry climate, the people down
here had to work slow, for short spells at a time, while
they actually put in about the same day's work as North
Americans, who did all their work in a bunch and then
took their well-deserved rest in another unbroken stretch,
instead of working and resting round the clock in what
seemed catnaps and short bursts of energy to an Anglo.

But while his men's lifestyle was pragmatic and probably the only way one could hope to reach old age down
here, he wanted to teach them new habits at least for the
time being. He knew *other* military or quasi-military
leaders south of the Texas line campaigned as they'd been
brought up, and, on more than one occasion, Captain
Gringo had stolen a march on his enemy for the moment
by skipping la siesta or leaving the adelitas behind so his
men would be moving when local custom dictated that
they should be fornicating.

The cooler highland night helped. He'd noticed before
how Latins tended to cling to tropic-lowland habits even
when they moved to a more reasonable climate. It *wouldn't*
kill you to put in twelve hours of anything sensible, with
the thermometer below seventy. So when some of his
weaker sisters sobbed out pathetically from time to time
along the trail that he was killing them, he just told them
they'd never had it so good and kept them moving. He felt
sure that all the real sissies had deserted by now, and when

some of the gripers started adding threats to his life as they bitched about the pace, he knew he was right. Soldiers who bitched openly when it didn't matter could usually be depended on when it did.

The bitching sounded more like wolves howling when the full moon passed the midnight zenith and he said not one word about anyone getting any sleep at all tonight. But they got a break, or he gave them one, when trade-swept clouds began to cover the moon along about 3:00 A.M. and he ordered a sack call until dawn.

They spread their blankets in a grove of highland live oak, too beat to jerk off or pay much attention to the plum-sized acorns they were lying on. So at sunrise, when he called out cheerfully, "Drop your cocks and grab your socks! Let's get it on the road!" they rose, if not bright-eyed and bushy-tailed, well rested by the short naps they were used to in any case.

Captain Gringo saw that his forced march had paid off when, less than an hour into the day, they reached the old stage route Celia had told them about.

Captain Gringo called in his noncoms for a consultation, standing in the center of the crossroads surrounded by more live oak. He pointed north and said, "I'm taking a corporal's squad up that way to check out that Indian bridge site that shouldn't be far. I want the trails east, west, and south secured by a rifle squad out at least a hundred meters and dug in on either side, well spread. I want the rest of the outfit hidden in the oaks till I get back. Lieutenant Verrier here is in command till I do. Any questions?"

Gaston said, "Oui. Are you leaving the machine gun with me, Dick?"

"Of course. The old bridge up that way is supposed to be out. I just want to make sure. You guys are more likely to have company than me. Any other questions?"

A sergeant asked, "Sí, Captain Gringo. For why do we have to secure the trail we just came down? The only people back that way are on *our* side, no?"

"No. Have you forgotten that original trail we left to follow this one east?"

The sergeant blushed becomingly and said, "Forgive me. It is said they dropped me on my head many times when I was a baby."

Captain Gringo smiled thinly and said, "Welcome to the club." Then he pointed to a guerrilla holding more or less a corporal's rank and said, "Rivera. You and yours. Let's go."

Then he turned and started up the trail leading more or less north, not looking back. He didn't have to. Rivera and his squad crunched pretty good on the oak-littered and obviously disused trail.

As the rain forest inched in from either side to reclaim the cleared and hard-beaten soil, the erstwhile thoroughfare narrowed to a path they had to follow Indian-file. But here and there he spotted a giant acorn with its rotting side up or a presumptuous low branch someone had sort of discouraged with a fairly fresh machete chop. So he called softly back to Rivera, "Heads up. Someone still *uses* this path on occasion. Probably local Indians. How do you get along with Guaymi, Corporal?"

Rivera said, "Not very well. But my sainted grandfather always said to leave them alone if they left me alone."

Rivera's grandfather had no doubt given good advice. But it suddenly became a little difficult to follow when, ahead on the narrow path, a trio of thoughtful-looking Indians materialized.

They wore peon straw sombreros and the long white cotton gowns of their Maya cousins to the north. They were apparently armed only with walking sticks, or clubs. So Captain Gringo knew they had more seriously armed backup watching from the brush all around.

He stopped, smiled, and raised his empty right hand in the universal peace sign that seemed to work with most American Indians. Then he said, "Utz-in puk-siqual!" which seemed to work best with most Maya speakers.

The oldest and most officious-looking Guaymi tried not

to look surprised and replied, in Spanish, "My heart is good, too, if that was what you just tried to say, Señor. I, too, know a little of the Mam Ob speech, albeit, forgive me, you speak it strangely. Would you mind if we spoke Spanish?"

"I was *hoping* you spoke Spanish, Jefe. I run out of things to say in the Grandfather Talk once I use up 'ma' and 'bei.' "

The older Indian smiled thinly and said, "It is surprising how far one can get with a woman only knowing 'yes' and 'no.' Was it a Guaymi *maiden* who taught you so much, Señor?"

Captain Gringo hastily assured him of his profoundest respect for Guaymi maidens, adding that in fact he'd never met one, let alone gotten her to teach him anything her elders might or might not have approved of.

This was the simple truth. He'd learned his few Maya words and a lot about Maya sexual activity from that lush little gal up Tehuantepec way, and they said the Guaymi were no closer related to true Maya as, say, Spanish or Italians.

The only Guaymi who seemed in a mood to speak to him at all, friendly or otherwise, nodded soberly and asked, "In what way can we be of service to you, Señor . . . ?"

"Walker. Ricardo Walker. I am also called Captain Gringo, for some reason."

The jefe smiled more pleasantly this time, as he nodded and said, "The reason seems obvious to me, and we have *heard* of you, Captain Gringo! A man's reputation spreads fast, when it is said he has a good heart indeed, even to despised Indians. Are you planning to overthrow the government or simply raid for plunder in these parts? In either case, count us *in!* We have heard what you did for the Mosquito and San Blas tribes. Though I am, myself, a Cristiano, most of the time, I do not argue when the old ones suggest you could have been sent by the elder god, Ah-Puch, for to help los pobrecitos Indios!"

Captain Gringo chuckled and said, "Next revolution, maybe. Right now I'm trying to help *all* the little people of Costa Rica. You've heard, of course, about the troubles to the south?"

"Sí. That is for why we have moved back up here to our old hunting grounds. When you people fight each other, it is a good idea for Indians to get out of the way. Not speaking of yourself, personally. I hope they wipe each other out."

Captain Gringo turned and said to Rivera, "Corporal, take your squad back to the crossroads and tell Lieutenant Verrier I may be a little late and not to get excited."

"Do you think that would be wise, Captain Gringo?"

"If I didn't think it was wise I wouldn't tell you to *do* it. *Move!*"

Rivera did, calling out, "Vamanos, hombres!" as he got himself and his men out of there as fast as he could. As soon as Captain Gringo found himself alone with the Indians, and not as happy about it as he might be letting on, he took out a claro, lit up, and handed it to the jefe, who took it, puffed it soberly, and said, "You are a trusting man, for one of *them*."

Captain Gringo said, "I am not one of them. I am a Yanqui. That is why I sent them away, so we could talk."

The old Indian brightened and said, "Bueno. What kind of treachery are we planning, Captain Gringo?"

The tall American laughed and said, "Look, we both know the Costa Rican government gives everyone a better deal than that military junta running Colombia and the isthmus to the south would, Jefe."

"The blancos from San José call us lazy Indians and cheat us on the price of our forest products."

"That's what I just said. Colombia has San Blas diving for pearls at gunpoint whether they can swim or not. Colombian regulars are headed this way with guns and hard-ons to eat all your women and rape all your chickens. So what's it going to be, Jefe, Costa Ricans who don't

really give a shit about you one way or the other, or
Colombians who still keep Indian slaves?''

The jefe took a long, thoughtful drag on the claro before
handing it back and asking, ''What do you want us to
do?''

''First, show me to that old bridge. I sent the others
away not because I'm mad at them but because I like to
have an occasional card up my sleeve, and when a guy
deserts or gets captured, you just never know who he'll be
chatting with.''

The jefe shrugged and said, ''Follow us, then. But I do
not think the bridge will be of any use to you or anyone
else in its present condition. It has not been kept in a state
of repair since the government built that new steel span to
the west.''

Captain Gringo had to follow them only a quarter mile
to see that the jefe had spoken the simple truth and then
some.

He stared out across the yawning canyon at the two
strands of frayed rope sagging deeply in the middle over
the milling white water even farther below. The catwalk
that had once hung between the remaining cables wasn't
there these days, save for a plank still waving in the
canyon breezes as it hung straight down from a thinner line
attached to the main ones. He nodded soberly and told the
jefe, as if he had to, ''No way anyone's about to cross here
now. How long do you think it would take to string a new
walkway, Jefe?''

The old Indian shrugged and replied, ''Quién sabe? We
were not the ones who built it and kept it in repair.
Another band, on the far side, used to charge modest tolls
for crossing their bridge. *They* could no doubt repair it in a
few weeks, assuming those main cables are still sound,
and there was any way for to *ask* them to, from here. I do
not know if they are even there now. They have no reason
to be, now that they are no longer in the bridge business.
Those trees across the canyon are not oak. So the hunting
over there is poor, eh?''

"Don't you people have ways of signaling one another, Jefe?"

"For why? I told you they were not of our band. The elder gods gave them that side of the canyon as they gave us *this* side. The bridge was built by Indians, it is true. But for blanco travelers, with money, not for the use of people who know enough to stay on their own hunting grounds and avoid needless machete fights with strange bands, eh?"

Captain Gringo shrugged and said, "Okay, even negative military intelligence is still military intelligence. If nobody can cross here, nobody can cross here. Muchas gracias, Jefe. You've been a great help."

As he turned away from the truly gut-wrenching as well as dismal view, the old jefe asked, "Do you wish for my band to join you and kill those invaders, Captain Gringo?"

He shook his head and said, "You people may be in enough trouble, if my better-armed men and me can't stop 'em, Jefe. If they get through *us*, they'll be coming at *you*, and your people have no line of retreat! You'd better move your band west to the remaining bridge and cross over to the safer side."

"That is not possible, Captain Gringo. This is where we have our scattered corn milpas and little houses, humble as they may be. This is our land. This is where we stay. This is what we stand ready to fight to the last for, against all comers!"

"I'd better get moving, then. Because those motherfuckers sure are coming, and if I can't stop 'em with modern weapons, you and your machetes had sure as hell better be *good!*"

Back at the crossroads, Captain Gringo found more people than he'd expected. Gaston was holding a couple of guys at gunpoint even though one held a drooping white flag on a recently cut stick. They were unarmed but otherwise looked pretty bandito in their big vaquero hats and greasy charro outfits trimmed with silver conchos. As Captain Gringo approached, Gaston called out, "Eh bien, we were just talking about you. These innocent-looking wayfaring strangers want to wayfare past us, which seems reasonable, but they also say they have a large armed band to the east in the woods, waiting to see how this truce talk goes, which does not."

Captain Gringo moved in to ask the truce party what it had to say for itself. The one who must have been boss, since he made the other guy carry the flag, smiled jovially and replied, "I am called el Arbitrador, because, as anyone in these parts can tell you, my muchachos and me keep peace between the villages and assure safe travel on the roads at night."

"At a price, of course?"

"Naturally. It is hard work for to do so much good for mankind. But this unpleasant little friend of yours here has no right to call us bandits and, for some odd reason, camels?"

Gaston said, "Mais non, I have every right in the world to call you anything, since I have you covered by a machine gun and beaucoup rifles."

El Arbitrador sighed and said, "I reproach you, Señor. Is that any way to speak to anyone who approaches you unarmed under a truce flag?"

Captain Gringo said, "He calls *me* lots of names, too. You want a truce talk, you can have a truce talk. So start talking and, oh, by the way, that jacket's a little snug if you're trying to *hide* that .45 tucked in your sash, Amigo."

El Arbitrador laughed easily and replied, "What's a little gun among friends, eh? The deal I offer is this. Why should coyotes hunt each other when the world's so filled with sheep? My boys and me just brushed with Colombian regulars a few days to the south, and we never wish for to go through *that* again. It is my wish only to keep going north, away from the battle zone. Is that too much for to ask?"

"How many of you are there, with how many guns?"

"No more than three hundred, counting our adelitas. I hide nothing from you, Captain Gringo, since I have heard of you and would as soon fight the Colombians. Our adelitas may have a few guns as well. This is a tough neighborhood. But none of us are looking for a fight. We only wish for to somehow cross over into safer parts. With your permissión, of course."

Captain Gringo nodded and said, "That sounds reasonable. We have more important people to fight, too. You and yours can't use the old Indian bridge anymore. It's not there now, but a lot of truculent Guaymi still are, and their jefe just told me they don't trust any strangers. So here's what you'd better do. Wait till I swing my column south. I mean *wait*, like at least half an hour, then lead your column from that east road and follow that one, there, leading to the steel bridge at Molina del Diablo. How do you like it so far?"

"Much better than fighting people armed with machine guns. Does a Maxim really spit six hundred rounds a minute, Captain Gringo?"

"Try to pull a fast one and you'll find out. Here comes the part you might not like. I'm working for the government this season. So I've got others covering the crossing at Molina del Diablo with other machine guns and a mountain mortar. They're not going to let you cross to the other side bearing arms. Those are the orders I left with them, see?"

El Arbitrador looked unhappy and asked, "Could you not give us a note, making an exception in our case, Amigo?"

"Not even if I wanted to. I've got orders, too, from San José. If Costa Rica wanted armed men streaming north through the coffee trees, they wouldn't have hired us to make sure that just couldn't happen. As war refugees, you're free to cross the bridge. As armed whatever, you're not. It's as simple as that."

The one who'd been silently holding the truce flag all this time growled deep in his throat and asked his leader,

"Are you going to let this lousy gringo talk to you like that, jefe?"

El Arbitrador kicked his ankle and said to Captain Gringo, "You must forgive him. He has never been right in the head since that mule stepped on it. Those of us endowed with brains at birth can see when we may or may not have a choice. If we have your permission to rejoin our friends, you have *my* word we shall avoid unfriendly contact with your column here. We shall make no move until you are well on your way, eh?"

Captain Gringo nodded and they turned away. As they were still within earshot, the one with the flag asked, "What about the bastards at that bridge crossing?" before his leader could punch him to shut him up.

Captain Gringo nodded at Gaston and said, "That's that. Let's get the show on the road."

"You know, of course, they mean to discuss the matter further with Dutch and the others at the crossing?"

"Let 'em. If they haven't got the weight to take us on in the open, they're not about to cross that bridge one minute before old Dutch wants 'em to, and, if they even spit at Dutch, he's not going to *want* 'em to."

So, a few minutes later they were on their way south along the old stage route, maybe. Captain Gringo marched his men well clear of the crossroads, marched them a bit farther to make sure they weren't being followed, then called a halt, called in his scouts, and announced, "New route, hombres. We're forging due east through the trees. The minute the point hits the other north–south road, he's to dig in and send his getaway back with the news. What are you all waiting for? Don't you know how it's done *yet?* Move!"

They did. Gaston waited until the column was threading its way through mixed live oak and highland pine before asking, "How do you know there's another main trail to the east, Dick? Have you been hiding a crystal ball under your hat all this time?"

Captain Gringo said, "Just a few brains. Those owl

hoots were following the east–west wagon trace, looking for a crossing, when they stumbled into us from the *east,* right?''

"Oui. So what?''

"So el Arbitrador said he and his people had brushed with Colombians and headed *north.* How the fuck could they have done so along the stage route hitting that crossroads from the *south?*''

Gaston nodded as he observed, "Oui, I must be getting old. But this is still most inconsiderate of you, my boisterous youth. We could have opted for that first road running south. We could have opted for the second road running south, but no, you insist on enjoying the wonders of the *third* route south, on which the Colombians are no doubt coming *north!* Why do you do things like that, Dick? Have you a special fondness for noise?''

Captain Gringo laughed and said, "Relax. I told you this was only a patrol. I just want to locate the bastards, not brush with a whole column of regulars, if it can be avoided.''

"Sacre God damn, if you would listen to your elders, I could *tell* you how to avoid it! Mais non, you keep insisting on marching the wrong way! What is there to find out, worth the risk to our adorable derrieres, now? We know they have crossed the border because they have started chasing people on this side of the border. We know which way they are coming. We know there is no way to stop anyone at all serious on this side of that canyon and . . .''

"We know no such thing,'' Captain Gringo cut in, adding, "There may be another natural ambush further south. Even if there isn't, we might be able to slow them some. Meanwhile, other refugees trying to escape along the roads the pricks *aren't* advancing along could use the extra *time,* see?''

"I see you are fibbing to your elders again, you hairy-chested brute! How on earth do you mean to even slow them down without, as you say, *brushing* them? Mon

Dieu, what a quaint way to put hosing people down avec machine-gun fire. What would you call artillery fire, sweeping?"

"If we had any real artillery, I'd call it booting them out of the country. But we don't have anything but that pissy little mortar they probably have outranged with their big guns. So we'll just have to do what we can with what we have, right?"

"God damn it, Dick, you just said you were hoping to *avoid* serious contact with the enemy!"

"I know, I know, but I didn't *promise* anything, if anything tempting turns up ahead. Come on, God damn it, you can walk faster than that."

They heard the road before they saw it. When the refugees streaming north under all they could carry and all the red dust they could raise with their hurried footsteps spotted Captain Gringo and his men, they got even noisier, dropping their bundles and raising their hands or skirts, depending.

Captain Gringo reassured the frightened peones and instructed them how to reach the only bridge across the canyon to the north. They in turn instructed him regarding the situation to the south. It wasn't good. So far, to be fair, the Colombian regulars seemed to be spending most of their energy flushing out bandits and rebels they'd chased across the border. But the prudent Costa Rican campesinos were still for the most part voting with their feet to remain under Costa Rican rule.

Captain Gringo led his column south along the edge of the trail, single file, stopping a refugee now and again to ask if they knew just *where* the nearest invaders were. All anyone seemed able to tell him was that wherever they were, they were too close for comfort. The border they'd jumped was a little over a day's march to the south. So at least the advance scouts of the invading army had to be closer than that. Much closer than that.

About an hour down the road, the stream of refugees turned to a trickle and then the road was clear ahead as far as they could see. So Captain Gringo called a halt, waved his leaders together, and told them, "Something's blocking traffic ahead. Until we find out it's not just a pothole, we'll be moving abreast in a line of skirmish, half of our riflemen to the right, the other half on my left flank. I'm taking the road, very very carefully, with the machine gun. Any questions?"

"Sí, Captain Gringo. What do you think we shall find ahead of us?"

"If I knew that, I wouldn't have to move very very carefully. Let's move it. Get your dress on me and keep it. If I go down, Lieutenant Verrier here is in command. If he goes down, get your men back to the main outfit as best you can and tell Captain Lansford something *awful* is coming at him. You have your orders. What are you waiting for?"

As the guerrilla leaders fanned out to line up their followers as told, Captain Gringo signaled the private who'd been packing the Maxim up to now and said, "Give me that and grab some ammo boxes. Then stay as close to me as you can without stepping on my heels. I want the rest of the machine-guns squad covering us, close, but out to either side."

He took the Maxim and opened the petcock to drain the water jacket in case he had to do some broken field running with the heavy-enough-as-it-was weapon. Then he moved on with the Maxim over his shoulder like a rifle, pissing oily water on the red dust behind him.

Gaston fell in beside him, asking if he thought he'd need help with the belts. Captain Gringo said, "No. Not if this squad we spent so much time training paid any attention at all. If we run into anything interesting, I'll hit the dirt, and my fire ought to keep them interested if not pinned down. Our skirmishers on the right should freeze in place as they wait for further orders. So if you're out on the left to lead them in a flanking attack . . .''

"Mais oui, my fiendish child," Gaston cut in, adding with a fiendish cackle of his own, "Since the book says to expect us to wheel our *right* flank nine times out of ten . . .''

"God damn it, Gaston!"

"I'm going, I'm going. I just wanted to tell you how much I adored you on the way out the door. Good hunting and, ah, be careful, Dick."

Captain Gringo didn't answer. Gaston was always offering uncalled-for advice. The gun was lighter now as the wary American moved ahead carefully indeed, keeping to the grassy edge of the trail and, each time he came to a bend, shifting the Maxim to port arms long enough to check out the next stretch with the armed machine gun looking the same direction he was.

It seemed a long time but was probably no more than an hour before he spotted the roadblock ahead. A couple of heavy wagons had been placed broadside to block the trail where it cut through a rocky ridge of old cooled lava. Riflemen sat perched like vultures on the black rock at either side of the gap under those big floppy sombreros ladrónes seemed to find so romantic. Other dramatically dressed figures lounged around the wagons as, on the far side, some sort of negotiations Captain Gringo couldn't quite make out were going on.

He saw that the roadblockers were moving one of the wagons out of the way. So he moved back around the bend with his own guys and, sure enough, in a little while five horse-drawn carriages appeared, going at a good clip, as if in a hurry to put some distance between themselves and the gang that had just shaken them down. Captain Gringo waved them down. But they must not have had any more loose change. The drivers cursed him and whipped their teams faster, which was a pretty dumb thing to do when anyone could see the big Yank was packing a machine gun. But he let it pass, and a few minutes later an ox cart going too slow to argue came around the bend.

He stopped it. The prosperous but dusty and bedraggled-looking campesino family in the cart looked sadly at him, and the man leading the oxen sighed and said, "As God is my witness, Señor, we gave your friends around the bend all we had."

Captain Gringo said, "Stick around and you may get it back. I just stopped you to make sure of something. How many in the gang and what's their story?"

The older man looked suddenly relieved and replied, "I counted no more than a dozen rifles pointed directly at us. They may have more in the rocks to either side. They say they are collecting a road tax for the government for to help defend our country. I did not consider it wise at the moment to doubt them."

"Bueno. One more question. Are there many innocent bystanders on the road behind that barricade?"

"Sí, Señor. They will not let anyone through who will not give them ten colónes a head and a hundred for each vehicle. Not many people have that kind of money, so, sí, the road beyond is most crowded. The pobrecitos have no other place to go. The ladrónes won't let them go on. They are afraid to go back where they came from, because of the invaders, so . . ."

"I get the picture, Señor. Take your family around the next bend and pull off into the woods. How much did they get from you?"

"Alas, sixty for the heads of me and my family, a hundred for this old cart I could not sell for half as much."

"Right. You're probably due a little interest for the loan. Don't come to withdraw it just because you hear some noise. I'll send one of my men to you with your money, if we win."

"El Señor is muy simpático. I am called Diego Garcia y Moreno, and my family and me shall live for the day we can repay your kindness!"

Captain Gringo knew that when an Hispanic told you

what he was called, you were supposed to tell him what
you were called. So he identified himself, and when he
did, the campesino nodded and said it figured.

As the ox cart moved on, Captain Gringo told one of his
men to run over and freeze their right flank. He knew
Gaston played well by ear. So he moved off the road to the
left and worked his way toward the rocks on that side of
the roadblock.

The bandits didn't spot him. They weren't supposed to.
But Gaston sent young Pepe to join him, asking what was
up. He told the youth, "By now Lieutenant Verrier knows.
Stick close to me. Keep your head up, your ass down, and
your mouth shut. See that rocky ridge ahead through the
trees? Okay, I may need a boost getting me and this
Maxim up to the crest. After that, the form's pretty
basic."

He led the advance, or tried to, until Pepe gasped and
said, "I see one of the bastards, up on the ridge!" which
was a sensible thing to say. Then he gushed, "I'll get
him!" which wasn't true, as, suiting actions to words, the
overactive but not at all bright Pepe dashed forward to
scale the black rocks behind the seated lookout.

The lookout didn't stay seated the other way long, as he
heard Pepe scrambling up to join him. He pivoted on one
buttock and blew Pepe away with the rifle held across his
thighs. Then *he* got blown off the far side of the ridge as
Captain Gringo, cursing them both, charged forward with
the Maxim braced on one hip, spitting lead!

Ignoring the dead boy for the moment, Captain Gringo
took the same route up the steep rocky slope, then ran
along the ridge with the trailing machine-gun belt lashing
behind him like the tail of an angry cat as he fired short
but deadly bursts at anyone who wanted to argue about it.

Not many did. He blew the other lookout on his side
ass-over-teakettle down into the roadblock. Then he put a
short long-distance burst into the buzzard on the far side
before he could decide whether to fire back or duck.
Captain Gringo fired the last of his belt in a long withering

burst at the ladrónes dumb enough to still be on the road when he reached it. Then the Maxim choked on an empty chamber. Which was just as well, since he'd be wasting ammo trying to gun the survivors at that range as they ran like hell into the woods on the far side.

A withering crackle of rifle fire told them and Captain Gringo what a dumb move *that* had been, as the fleeing bandits migrated like ducks along the right skirmish line's field of fire and, of course, didn't make it to their nesting grounds that season after all.

As Captain Gringo stood on the rocks, snatching a fresh belt from his loader to rearm the Maxim, he could see all the people on the south side of the ridge who'd been blocked from safe passage north. For some reason, lots of women were blowing kisses at him and lots of men were throwing their sombreros in the air. As he looked for an easy way down, Gaston joined him to say, "Spoilsport. My children and me never got to fire a shot. Let me count the ways I love you. I see, two, four, eight, sixteen, seventeen of the cochons down there in no condition to annoy anyone at the moment. You left another one back there on the far side of these rocks, très messy. Not a bad days work, non?"

"It could have been better. We lost Pepe, or he lost himself. So *him*, at least, we gotta bury right. Let's get those corpses and wagons out of the way so all those poor slobs can move on. From the looks of that crowd, the border-jumping Colombians can't be far *behind* them!"

As they followed the road south it got broader and the country on either side opened wider, too. They passed small milpas of subsistence crops, mostly the mestizo triad of corn, beans, and squash, with larger areas given over to cash crops of coffee and red peppers. They were too high in the hills for bananas or sugarcane. The few clusters of houses they passed were deserted. There were no signs of military activity, yet, but word seemed to be getting around.

As they marched toward the border, looking for a likely strong place to fortify, they became increasingly gloomy about the odds of finding one. The valley the road followed was opening wider, not narrowing, affording room for cavalry to maneuver and artillery to wheel. So when Gaston pointed out that this was hardly the sort of place to raise healthy young guerrillas to manhood, Captain Gringo didn't argue. He said, "Yeah, how do you like that rocky ridge back up the road?"

Gaston shook his head and said, "Those *bandits* did not do so well there against one machine gun and a handful of rifles. Trust an old artilleryman for once, Dick. We have a chance, only a chance, of stopping them at Molina del Diablo, if we blow the bridge in time. So why are we still walking the wrong way in this hot sun?"

Captain Gringo pointed with his chin at a tree line in the middle distance and said, "I want to make certain nobody's crowding us as we head back. Soon as we come to another broad open stretch, we will."

They trudged on. Then Captain Gringo raised a hand to halt the column and said, "See what I mean?" as one of his forward scouts appeared on the road, running back to them as if his life depended on it.

As the sweaty guerrilla slid to a dusty stop in front of them, Captain Gringo snapped, "Report!" and the scout said, "Beyond that coffee, camped in a fallow field, a band of gitanos, maybe even hadas, guarded by a big gray dragon, Captain Gringo!"

"Are you drunk, Soldado? Gypsies make sense. Fairies and dragons don't!"

"On my mother's honor, Señor! The others saw this strange business, too, and they are covering the fairy camp from the trees. Maybe they are not real fairies. Maybe they are just crazy gitanos dressed up funny with their carts painted most strange. But the *dragon,* at least, is real. I have never believed in dragons. But it is there. The strangest sight I have ever seen. Did you know dragons eat backwards? Perhaps that is how they manage not to burn the fodder as it goes down their flaming throats, no?''

"This I gotta see," said Captain Gringo, adding, "Gaston, move the guys on those trees in skirmish and do what you have to if I get eaten by any dragons."

Then he told the scout to come with him as he started jogging ahead. The scout fell in on his left, and as they made for the trees together he said, "Run that part about dragons eating backwards by me again. Dragons eating *forward* sound nutty enough, dammit!"

The scout panted as he said, "It is true, I swear. They have it staked out in the field for to graze as it guards them. It keeps pulling up grass with its tail and stuffing it up its asshole. Do not look at me like that, por favor. You will see this soon for yourself, and I confess I know nothing about dragon digestion. I did not even know they *ate* grass, let alone that they took it up the *ass!*''

They cut off the road and through the coffee plantation to join the other bewildered scouts lying flat along the tree line to watch dragons acting weird indeed in the open field beyond.

Captain Gringo, who'd no doubt seen more of the world than his backwoods followers, laughed like hell and said, "For God's sake, it's an *elephant,* you poor dumb bastards!"

As the elephant out in the field took another trunkful of grass, the scout who'd fetched him said, "I do not know what an elephant looks like, either. But whatever it is, there it goes stuffing grass up its ass again and, look, it is flapping its *wings!*''

Captain Gringo said, "Right. Looks like some sort of traveling circus. Cover me. I'd better go in and see what the fuck a little one-ring tent show's doing here, of all places!"

As he broke cover to cross the field, swinging wide of the staked and now-suspicious elephant as it snorted at him with its "tail," he saw that the "fairies" had noticed his approach too, and were popping out of the garishly painted wagons to stare nervously, although none of them seemed to be pointing guns his way.

A small, muscular-looking man in bright red tights advanced to meet him, calling out, "That is far enough, Señor. I mean no disrespect, but some of the freaks are uneasy around strangers."

Captain Gringo stopped and said, "That sounds fair. That guy coming up behind you makes me sort of nervous, too. Does he *really* have two heads or is that just his stage costume?"

The man in red turned to tell the two-headed freak, "José-José, go back and guard the women, you idiot-idiot. I shall deal with this."

As the freak shrugged, turned, and ran back to the wagon ring, the man in red said, "He only uses the brain in one of those heads, and in truth it is not a very bright one. I am Bombasto, the human cannonball. I am the only normal man left, now that the management has decamped with all the money and decent carriages, for to *strand* us here."

Captain Gringo stared past Bombasto at the heavy wagons and what looked like a big squat howitzer painted fire-engine red as he replied, "I think they passed us on the road to the north. Does that cannon really work?"

Bombasto shrugged and said, "It can fire me from one end of the big top to the other. If you mean, is it a real cannon, of course not. The explosive charge is just for show. I am actually propelled by a powerful spring catapult. But don't you dare call me a *fake!* How would *you* like to be shot out a cannon, even by springs, eh?"

"Not very much. Let me get this straight. You and the, ah, expendable members of your tent show have been left behind by the, ah, prosperous and able bodied?"

Bombasto curled his lip and said, "I was not left behind. I chose for to stay. It was monstrous to leave the freak show and poor old Isabel over there behind!"

"Is Isabel the elephant?"

"Sí. I have been planning for to have her haul at least

one wagon and my cannon, of course, as soon as she has recovered. We pushed hard, this far, and then, when neither poor Isabel or the weaker members of the troup could keep up, they left us here on our own.''

"Some guys are like that, when they have plenty of insurance. How far are we from the Colombian army right now, Bombasto?''

The human cannonball shrugged and said, ''Quién sabe? We were playing a town below the border in Panama when all hell broke loose. Since everyone who could started running, we thought it wise to do the same. It is said the regulars are arresting anyone who cannot show Colombian visas, and we never concerned ourselves with such matters before. We crossed the border, wherever that might be, well ahead of them. It is said they are making methodical sweeps, moving north like a big broom. We have not been looking forward to being swept up. You know how cruel even *unarmed* people can be to *freaks,* eh?''

"That's for damned sure. They probably have standing orders to shoot all suspicious characters, and *my* guys were suspicious as hell of you and yours just now. You're in a hell of a spot, aren't you?''

Bombasto shrugged and said, ''I have been killed before. Sometimes, no matter how one tries, one misses the net. I do not look forward to being killed again. But what else can a man do, eh?''

"A lot of guys would have run away by now. But you're right, Bombasto. You look like a man to me, too. You'd better introduce me to the others. We're going to have to put all the heads we have together, including José-José's, if we're going to get you all out of here in time.''

"You wish to help? Bueno, I can use all the help I can get. But what can just the two of us do, Señor? Many of the freaks simply cannot walk more than a few steps at a time, and they are the lucky ones.''

"I'm not alone. They call me Captain Gringo. I'm a soldier of fortune, leading plenty of guys who can carry someone piggyback, if they have to.''

"Ah, but what if they do not choose to? You know how some people feel about *any* freaks, and some of my friends are, ah, rather grotesque."

"We're wasting time, Bombasto. I said my muchachos can do what they have to, and when I tell 'em to, they have to."

The human cannonball nodded and took his arm to show the others they were pals as he led the tall American over to the wagons to meet the damnedest set of pathetic freaks of nature he'd ever seen all at once in one place. Even as a kid, he'd never enjoyed freak shows when the circus came to town. So he'd mostly fed the elephants and tried to get in to see the hootchy-kootchy shows along the midway.

José-José at least could walk, as could the troop of midgets if they didn't have to walk as fast as longer-limbed soldados. Neither the fat lady nor her husband, the human skeleton, looked in shape to make a forced march. It got worse when Bombasto introduced him to the human cater-pillar, the cruel joke nature had played on a sad-eyed girl born with a pretty face and a limbless, apparently boneless body encased in a terrycloth sack that made her indeed resemble some sort of monstrous insect larva, lying in a padded basket. The three-legged man, really still a boy, had indeed three legs as advertised. When Captain Gringo gravely shook his hand and asked him how well he could get around on his three withered limbs, he said not so good, but that he was willing to try. He didn't ask the siamese twins how they felt about ducking in unison. Obviously if one saw the need to duck in time but the other didn't, two pretty girls sharing one existence would cease to exist. The pinhead, an unfortunate Negro, didn't have enough going on in his tiny misshapen skull to discuss the matter with. Bombasto said the pinhead could run like crazy, but tended to run in *circles* unless someone held him by one hand. They said reassuring things to others in worse shape. Then Bombasto introduced him to what seemed a perfectly normal and indeed attractive young woman seated on a crate inside a heavy robe for the time of day. Her name was Carlota. Her bleached blond hair clashed a bit with her Latin features, but she seemed otherwise normal and, when she spoke, intelligent. He asked, "How come *you* didn't run off with the others, Carlota? Wouldn't they take you with them?"

She shrugged and said, "I could have gone. I did not choose to. My place is here, with the other freaks."

"I hope you won't take this as an insult, Carlota. But you don't look like a freak to me."

She rose from her seat and said, "Sure I do," as she opened her robe. Under it, she was stark naked and built like a Greek goddess. But her lush curves were covered, collar bones to ankles, with a mosaic of tattoos, some of them sort of pornographic. He managed not to laugh at the grotesque, gnomish face using her pubic hair for a beard. Instead he nodded as if she'd just shown him an interesting art collection, which she had, in a way, and said, "All right. So you're a self-appointed freak. You still could have left the real ones behind. So fess up, aren't you a man like Bombasto here?"

The tattooed lady laughed, a bit bitterly, and wrapped up again as she said, "That's *one* thing I've never been called before. But all right, what can us *men* do to save my friends? They *are* my friends, no matter what *you* think of them!"

Captain Gringo said, "For openers, you can take that chip off your shoulder, Carlota. Then we'd better see about getting them the hell out of here, right?"

They did, but it was sort of complicated. Captain Gringo waved his scouts in and sent a runner for Gaston and the others. By the time he had some manpower to work with, he'd worked out some details with Bombasto. The elephant could haul one box wagon and the big but mostly sheet metal "cannon" that Bombasto insisted on hanging on to until he could get another job with hopefully nicer management. The others, of course, were entitled to such small treasures as they had. So after they'd dumped out most of the circus gear, the box wagon was still overloaded with costumes, mementos, and the special foods and medicines some of the more unfortunate required just to stay alive. The fat lady took up more than her fair share of space. Her husband said he was willing to walk, but, though he was a human skeleton, his screwed-up glands required an awesome load of special dietary crap in heavy cans and bottles. A couple of the semicrippled and helpless cases had to ride in the wagon. That still left some out. So Captain Gringo told his men what had to be done, and they, in turn, more than rose to the occasion.

His men were illiterate, superstitious peasants. They'd been raised to guard against the evil eye and watch out for spooks when going out to the woodpile after dark. They'd been taught that freaks of nature were the acts of a just God, as punishment for sins they could scarcely imagine, since they all knew at least one or two guys who'd slept with their sisters, and nothing much had happened to *them* or their children. Yet, with native grace, as the stranded freak show moved out behind the ponderous Isabel, those men picked up the lighter freaks and all the midgets, then carried them as gently, and as kindly, as they would have carried their own children.

In no time at all, the naturally dubious unfortunates and their newfound friends were getting along just fine. So, all that was left to worry about was the army chasing them. Old Isabel, though powerful, moved slow as hell.

Sunset caught up with them in a wooded area as the trades swept in an overcast that could have spelled rain and for sure meant a dark, moonless night ahead. So they moved well off the trail among the trees, and Captain Gringo put out twice as many pickets as he might have with only his well-armed men to worry about. Some of the people treated unkindly by nature not only had to eat special diets but had to eat them cooked. He ordered the campfires laid in shallow draw through the woods and told everyone to build them big and blazing while there was, hopefully, time, and then to let them die down to beds of coals that, while hot enough, wouldn't throw much light above the rims of the draw.

Since they'd be stuck there all night, and probably catching rain before morning, he gave permission to erect substantial lean-tos. He noted with considerable approval that his rough guerrillas not only got right to it, but built for the more helpless first. A trio of hardcase hombres who looked as if they'd murder a priest for his shoes soon had the human caterpillar snugly nestled in a bed of tender pine boughs under a tiny but stoutly built and rainproof canopy. Sheltering the fat lady took a bit more doing, even with her skinny husband's pathetic help. But before their supper was cooked they had everyone but the elephant well sheltered for the night.

Captain Gringo spread his own bedding under the lean-to built for him a little apart from the others on a rise where he and his Maxim could have a better view of things going boomp in the night. The machine gun was in its tarp, wedged under the low overhang where the lean-to's pine-thatched roofing met the ground. There was room to sit up the other way, of course. So he was seated there, almost finished with his coffee and beans, when Carlota, the tattooed lady, joined him.

Her robe gaped open a bit as she sat down beside him, unasked. But he'd already seen all she had to show, so what was a tit embellished with floral designs among friends, assuming they were friends? Carlota didn't look too friendly. She looked worried as she said, "I can't find the pinhead anywhere in camp. I'm afraid he's run away again or, more fairly, wandered off again. The poor thing hasn't the brains to be really naughty."

Captain Gringo shrugged, reached into his shirt for a

smoke, and told her not to worry, adding, "Our night pickets will pick him up if he wanders that far."

"What if he slips between the guards in this darkness?"

"I'll be mad as hell at them and he'll either come back or stay lost."

"But, Captain Gringo, the poor thing has no business wandering on his own when things are *calm!* He does not even know enough to feed himself when food is in front of him. How long do you think he could last on his own in a war zone?"

Captain Gringo lit the claro, blew a thoughtful smoke ring, then said, "Probably not as long as us. But *we're* not out of trouble yet by a long shot. I know it sounds cruel, Carlota, but we're going to have enough trouble keeping the ones who cooperate alive. So why worry about a guy too stupid to know he's getting killed in the first place? You're a little light complected to be his mother, aren't you?"

She smiled bitterly and replied, "I'll never be *anyone's* mother, now. No man who'd have me would be the sort I'd wish for to marry or, hell, even have an affair with."

He grimaced and said, "You must enjoy carrying crosses, Carlota. First you take on responsibilities nobody asked you to. Now you're weeping and wailing about your, ah, appearance. You were never *born* a freak. You're a pretty, nicely stacked dame who *chose* to be covered with tattoos, and, from the casual way you display your interesting art collection, you're not at all ashamed to show it off. What do you want from me, guilt? I don't remember drawing graffiti on *your* walls, Doll. So it must have been your idea to look sort of strange, and us guys get enough blame for things we never did from your less, ah, made-up sisters."

Carlota nodded sadly and said, "I know only too well I allowed myself to be made over into a circus freak. I do not even blame my late husband. I could have said no, and it was not his fault I lost my nerve. Had I been able to continue to perform up there . . . But why am I telling you all this? You've no doubt heard the same story in a million whorehouses, no?''

"I don't think I've been in anything like a *million* whorehouses, and I've seldom asked *any* lady why she chose to have that butterfly or rose tattoo, discreetly hidden by her skirt most of the time. I've never met any lady before who carried it to such an extreme. But if you don't want to tell me about it, don't. I hardly ever lose sleep over womanly notions of glamour. I gave up wondering about whalebone and punctured earlobes long ago, too.''

She must have wanted to tell him. She sighed and said, "How often I wish I'd stopped with pierced ears, or even the rosebud on my thigh I thought a harmless lark when first I ran away with the circus. Not this one you found me with. A *big* one. Three rings. So long ago, it all seems, now.''

He buckled down to smoking his claro as he let her get it off her tattooed chest. She'd been right about her story being banal enough at the start. The cliché tale about a bored, beautiful village girl running off with a handsome circus performer. In Carlota's case, a high-wire walker instead of the man on the flying trapeze. He'd taught her the act, when he wasn't screwing or beating her, and for a time they'd been big time, prancing about on the high wire under the traveling big top, all over Latin America and even Europe one time, she insisted wistfully.

Then the guy had taken a fall from the wire. A bad one. So, crippled, he'd had to fall back on working as a tattoo artist, while Carlota went on alone as high-wire walker and, according to her, as a star until, one night, as she put it, she lost her nerve.

She explained, "It was not as if I fell, like poor Juanito. I had no such excuse. I had never fallen or even thought of falling, until one hot night in Ciudad Mexico I went up the ladder, looked down, and simply could not step out on the wire. It was horrible, horrible! The crowd below was laughing and, even worse, whistling, as I stood there, frozen, with one slipper out on the wire and my hands

simply stuck, white knuckled, to the platform rigging. I
kept trying. I was so mortified I was willing to die. Right
there. But not *that* way. Any way but *falling!* I tried to
force myself, even knowing I would surely lose my balance now, as upset as I was. But my limbs refused to obey
me. My bladder refused to obey me. I stood there, trem-
bling, with bees buzzing around inside my hollow shell of
a body as urine ran down my tights until, mercifully, a
kind and no-doubt frightened clown came up the ladder for
to get me down. He had to hit me to make me let go. I
fainted. So I don't know how, in the end, they got me
down. But I knew I would never, never, go *up* again!''

Captain Gringo nodded soberly and said, ''Once, when
I was maybe eight or nine, my folks had given me a .22
for my birthday. I already knew how to shoot. My dad had
taught me to shoot pretty good before he decided I was old
enough for my own gun, as a matter of fact. I went out to
the wood lot to try it out. I spotted a rabbit. It didn't see
me. I lined up the sights. I *had* the damned rabbit at easy
range. I couldn't pull the trigger. I tried and tried and my
goddamned trigger finger just wouldn't do what it was
told! The stupid rabbit went on eating for a million years
while I followed its hops with the sights until, finally, it
sensed something was up and simply hopped out of range,
slow, like it was *teasing* me. I thought I'd gone nuts or,
even worse, turned into a sissy. I was ashamed to tell my
dad. I couldn't tell anyone, for a long time. But there was
this old guy, the town drunk as a matter of fact, who liked
to brag about all the hunting he'd done in his time. So I
finally told *him*. It would have been easier to tell him
about jerking off in the outhouse with a copy of the *Police
Gazette*. But he didn't laugh. He said what I'd had was
just buck fever, and that if I tried again it might not
happen. So I tried again. And he was right. I wound up
shooting half the squirrels and rabbits in Connecticut that
afternoon. I've never had buck fever since.''

Carlota nodded and said, ''My late husband told me
much the same thing. Perhaps, had I been able to walk the

wire one more time, as he ordered me to, I might have recovered my nerve. But I didn't. I simply could no longer force my body up the ladder anywhere *near* the wire!''

"So that was the end of your stardom on the high wire?"

"Sí. We needed more money than Juanito could make from tattooing the few sailors and silly boys who came to the midway in a bravo mood. I had to have another act. I had no other circus skills. But anyone can be a freak, if he or she puts her mind to it. So I let Juanito put his needle to me, and the rest is ancient history."

Captain Gringo unclenched his jaws with a deliberate effort and asked quietly, ''How did this Juanito get to be your *late* husband? Did some human being put an end to the son of a bitch?''

Carlota shook her head and said, "He just died. It was for to get the medicines he needed for to keep him alive after his fall that I let myself become a freak. I do not wish to speak ill of the dead. I loved him, perhaps in an unhealthy way, now that I look back. It was not until we buried him that I began to realize how little it really took for a healthy person like myself to survive on, alone. It was only when I realized how I would be alone, forever, now, that I regretted what we had done to get me a new act. You must understand, Juanito was desperate and perhaps a little crazy, too. He did not realize what a freak indeed he was making of me. He thought of himself as an artist, and, in his own way, he loved me. Had he lived, it would not have mattered what I looked like with my clothes off. Despite his crippled body he was still a most skilled lover. We desired nobody but one another. So . . . Never mind, it's all ancient history, as I said."

"How long's it been, Carlota?"

"Three years, since my husband died. Longer than that if you mean how long since we had sex. Towards the end, it was very bad."

"It must have been. And nobody's made a pass at you since?"

She made a wry face and said, "On the contrary. You've no idea what sort of offers a tattooed lady gets as she performs naked for red-faced grinning louts. Unfortunately, I am just too fastidious for group sex or a giggling vaquero anxious to win a bet from his friends as they *watch!*"

He said, "I'm not talking about the savages who come to see your art collection wiggle. I thought you circus folk searched closer to home for your, ah, social outlets."

She said, "We do. Even the siamese twins have a rather tireless as well as handsome clown for a lover, or at least they did until he ran off with the others. I suppose I could have taken up with more than one roustabout by now, had I been willing to accept being treated like Flora y Dora. As a port in the storm when none of the *townie* girls are willing. Unfortunately, I have a romantic as well as fastidious nature."

"Well, hang in there. The right guy's sure to come along, Carlota."

"Who's looking for Señor Recto, at this late date? I would settle for a lover with only one head, if he knew how to treat me like a woman instead of a *monster!*"

Captain Gringo didn't answer at first. The distant fires were only ruby beds of coals now, and they could barely see each other, which probably helped. He said cautiously, "I've known how to treat a woman as a woman for some time, Carlota. It's my own romantic nature that keeps me out of all those whorehouses. But before I say something stupid, I'd better mention I'm a knockaround guy who has to keep moving on."

Her voice was a husky whisper as she asked, "Do you have to move on right away? Aren't you going to be here at least for this one night?"

He took her in his arms and kissed her as they fell together side by side across the pine-bough-cushioned bedding. She kissed back with the skill, and desperation, of the lonely and now fully aroused young woman she really was. And as he slipped her robe off in the darkness, her lush body felt as nice as any other he'd felt up lately. But once he got inside her, it felt even better.

Far to the north, in San José, another young man was enjoying the evening less, as he looked up at the colonel and military-police team who'd just burst into his quarters without knocking. The junior officer, naked under his bunk bedding, sat up and saluted smartly. But he looked rather silly, considering the time and place, as he asked, "To what do I owe this unexpected honor, Colonel Vegas?"

The Costa Rican officer who'd recruited Captain Gringo and Gaston smiled coldly down as he replied, "A cartographer third class who just made first class drew my attention only a few minutes ago to a curious thing he noticed in the map drawers, Major. This most dedicated young *soldado* was straightening up the office after all the recent activity when he noticed something few would have, since how often does anyone open an old-map drawer dated two surveys back, eh?"

The major in the bunk looked sincerely puzzled as he licked his lips and muttered, "Map drawers, Colonel? I have little to do with map drawers. When I wish for to obtain a map, I ask for one and they issue it to me."

"True, although it is an office you have full access to, as a field-grade officer. But we are getting ahead of the story, or perhaps you already *know* it?"

"I assure you, Colonel, I have no idea what you are talking about. But if there is anything wrong, and I can help in any way . . ."

Colonel Vegas said, "I think you know more than me about the matter. I *know* you know more than the young and now-promoted cartographer could have when he brought it to my attention that a copy of our most-recent survey of the Molina del Diablo sector had somehow gotten into a file now holding little more than historical interest. I did not tell him why anyone would drop a new map in with old and useless ones. Enlisted men have no need to know about such matters. Shall I tell *you* what I think must have happened, Major?''

"I wish you would, Colonel. I have no idea how the maps got mixed up by a section I do not command.''

Vegas said, "I think you do. I think when I ordered you to supply those soldiers of fortune with a map of the area they are covering, you went to the map room and told the sergeant in charge, in your usually democratic fashion, that you would get the map out yourself. I think you deliberately opened the flat of stale maps. I think the sergeant noticed and gently corrected you, opening the flat of *corrected* surveys above, which of course would cover anything *below* for a moment. I think in that moment you graciously accepted the right map and then, as the sergeant turned away, slipped it into the out-of-date flat. You grabbed an out-of-date map with the same motion, and then of course shut both drawers. Who would have noticed as you walked out, waving a sheet that, while out-of-date, was on the same paper and printed with the same heading, eh? I—may God forgive me—never more than scanned the sector number before giving it to Captain Gringo in good faith. So your ruse worked. At the moment, our informal irregulars are floundering about in the dark down there, without knowledge of the existent road net below the bridge. If they follow the only old trail on that useless map, it will lead them only to a distant as well as abandoned mining operation. It gets *more* amusing if the enemy coming up either of the practical routes from the border cuts them off in a dead end. Are you amused, Major?''

The younger officer swung his bare feet to the floor as he protested, "I swear to you this is all a hideous mistake, Colonel.''

But Vegas said, "Sí, and you made it. Don't bother to get up. You are not going anywhere right now." Then he turned to one of his MPs and added, "Bring in the other prisoner.''

In the moment before that could be done, Vegas turned back to the now very nervous-looking major and said conversationally, "Before you make any more stupid statements, I have more on you than the mere fact that you, and no other officer, went to get that map for me. I have your *motive* as well. I *considered* a stupid but innocent mistake before I called the MPs, Major. It was difficult at first to figure out why a member of my staff would wish to see the mission of Captain Gringo fail. I knew it had to be more than simple jealousy. You are not a battalion leader despite your rank, and, even if you were, you and me both know there is simply no reserve battalion for you to gallantly save the day with. But the new teléfono is a marvelous invention. It can save so much time, as one asks many questions all about the capital, no?"

The major licked his lips again and said, "Anyone you could possibly call in San José would surely tell you I am a patriotic officer with a spotless record as well as a good family background, Colonel!"

Vegas nodded and said, "They did. Your high family connections, in fact, may present a problem. But your broker, as he was praising you to the skies and was no doubt trying to reassure me, told me you hold *stock* in that foreign timber syndicate that currently holds vast forest reserves in the disputed area!"

The major paled and asked, "Are you suggesting the timber interests I am connected with, most casually, are plotting against Costa Rica, Colonel?"

"Of course not. They probably haven't even heard of the situation this early in the game. But *you* had, Major. You knew that should the border wind up *north* of that timber, once the dust settles, cutting it and exporting it would have to be under Colombian, not Costa Rican, laws about such matters."

The major shrugged and asked, "What advantage would that give anyone in the trade?"

"Oh, my God, he's *caught* and he still wants to play games? Very well, you licker of Colombian boots! You and I both know Costa Rica forbids destructive forest practices and charges an export tax on our natural resources. Colombia is ruled from a junta in the highlands that is barely interested in anything this far north but the rights to that canal route everyone wants but nobody wishes to pay for. Colombia won't charge your syndicate more than a few local bribes if they want to cut down *people*, so far north. I have a modest head for figures. I can see how stock in a suddenly prosperous or even about-to-be suddenly prosperous timber syndicate will soar. So stop trying to lie your way out of it, you fool. All we have to worry about now are the political repercussions."

The MP he'd sent came back in with a small, frightened, and rather effeminate enlisted man. Colonel Vegas told the MPs, "Bueno, leave us now," as he drew his sidearm.

As soon as he was alone with the bewildered pair, he scowled at the private and said, "You know what the penalty for your no-doubt-amusing vice is in this man's army, don't you?"

"As God is my witness, Colonel, I was only tying my shoe in that alley when they caught me with that civilian, ah, taking a piss or something."

"You were wearing *boots* and that's not the way they tell it. But never mind. Just kneel down there by the major's bunk, por favor."

"You wish . . . you wish for me to suck an *officer*, Colonel?"

The major gasped and said, "See here, God damn it!" and leaped to his feet to stand naked by the bunk, red faced and too pissed to feel fear for the moment. So the colonel shrugged, said, "This will do," and shot them both.

As the uniformed but known homosexual's body sprawled across the naked form of the dead officer, Vegas stepped to the door, opened it, and called in one of the MPs. As he showed the uneasy-looking enlisted man his handiwork, Vegas said, "Can you believe it? They attempted to have unnatural relations right in front of me, Sergeant!"

The MP, who'd been a lance corporal up to now, nodded soberly and said, "Si, you told us you suspected them both, Colonel."

Vegas said, "Nonetheless, we're going to have to treat this business with, ah, *tact,* because of the major's aristocratic connections. *You* look like a wise old noncom, Sergeant. How would you suggest we announce this scandal to the newspapers?"

The MP shrugged and asked, "For why do we have to bother the newspapers with a scandal that would shame the poor pervert's family, Colonel? If it were up to *me,* the matter would simply go in the secret files for those few higher-ranking officers wishing to know just what happened here. I don't think anyone in the army would wish the matter to go *further,* eh?"

"I knew I could count on you, Sergeant. Hell, make that Master Sergeant while we're at it. I, too, like to save needless paperwork."

All Captain Gringo knew about scandalous sexual matters at the moment was that Carlota sure looked weird from the shoulders down, now that the moon had come out again. She'd whimpered in dismay when it had, just as he was putting it to her dog style. But he'd assured her she looked just great on her hands and knees with him long-donging the Battle of Granada. And it did look sort of sexy, for some reason, to see he was keeping the Spanish knights on her left buttock from attacking the assembled Moorish army on her right buttock as they crossed lances over his *own* action. He wanted to come old-fashioned, this time. So he rolled her over in the moonlight as she covered her floral breasts with her tattooed forearms and begged him not to look too closely at what he was doing now. He couldn't resist. What man could have? He managed neither to gag nor to laugh as he looked down and saw that he was getting a blow job from a bearded gnome as well as a really great lay.

He fell forward as he felt he was almost there. She wrapped her arms around him, pressing her tattooed tits against his chest as if to hide them, and raised her knees and locked her shapely albeit strange-looking legs around his waist to come with him. When they came up for air, she sighed and said, "Oh, you *are* most romántico! I was so afraid you would not wish for to kiss me as we climaxed together just now."

He kissed her again before he chuckled and said, "That would be pretty stupid as well as rude, Doll. There's nothing wrong with your kissing equipment. Your face looks pretty as hell in the moonlight."

"I wish the moon would go away and never come back." She sighed, adding, "It is not just that I am covered with somewhat strange designs. Some of the words are dirty. Can you read them in this light?"

"No," he lied, wondering why even a nutty tattoo artist would have labeled one perky nipple *hot* and the other *cold* when they were both most obviously hot as hell. She said, "I am glad. I did not know what he'd written in that arrow pointed at my, ah, rear entrance, until I saw it in a double mirror one night and cried myself to sleep."

He said, "I didn't notice. I was too busy to read," as she snuggled closer to him with a contented sigh. He was glad he'd fibbed. He could see how it might disturb a sensitive woman like Carlota to have an arrow with a sign reading: THIS WAY TO THE PERFUME FACTORY pointed at her asshole, even when she hadn't been eating beans.

She was crying now, if his naked chest was any judge of tears. He knew better than to ask any woman in bed what the hell she was crying about. But it seemed the thing to do tonight, for some reason. Carlota sobbed as she said, "I am sorry. I know we agreed for to share only this night without thinking of tomorrow, Deek. But even a freak has dreams, and I can't help but wonder what the future holds in store for us now."

Enough was enough, God damn it, so he pulled no punches as he told her truthfully but gently, "The future holds damned little for *us,* as an even semipermanent plural. If we live through the next few days, *you'll* go on, *I'll* go on, but, as I told you before, I'm a knockaround guy, and any woman making permanent plans I'm included in is really a freak."

She didn't answer. He was afraid he'd hurt her more than he'd intended to. But as he held her closer to comfort her, she said, "In God's truth, I have not felt this normal since I can't remember when. Do you think we could make love some more, if I helped you with my, ah, mouth?"

He laughed and said, more to himself, in English, "The poor gnome might get jealous and I sure wouldn't want to get bitten," as he rolled her on her back again.

She looked up at him adoringly and asked, "What are you talking about, Querido?"

He said, "Never mind. Inside joke," as he put it back inside her.

She closed her eyes and hissed, "Oh, qué dulce y qué magnífico! How is it a man so well endowed and so passionate can treat a woman so sweetly, Deek?"

He muttered, "It ain't easy," as he tried to ignore all those gnomes, dragons, and creatures he had no names for, watching him lay her.

The only thing that could be said for moving out so slowly after sunrise was that people less burdened kept overtaking the column with fresh news as well as faster footwork.

It was definite now. The Colombians were coming up the road they were on, and, even allowing for some caution in strange territory, they couldn't be poking along behind an antique elephant.

Captain Gringo and his guerrillas couldn't abandon the

slow-moving circus folk, or at least didn't choose to, and Bombasto said there was no use hitting the elephant, as it would simply confuse her and she'd be as likely to lie down as to move faster. So it was with more than a little relief that he spotted the crossroads closest to the canyon ahead.

But when they reached it, people were crossing it the wrong way. He stopped an old man leading a burro and said, "Señor, the bridge is the *other* way, see?"

But the old man kept urging his overladen burro east as he replied, "There are banditos that way, too! Many banditos! They have taken over an abandoned estancia to use as a fortress and they refuse to let anyone pass who can't pay them with money or, if a woman, with other favors. The road that way is blocked even before one reaches the terrible people blocking it, Señor. Refugees by the hundreds are milling about to the west, afraid to move this way, unable to move the other way! I know of a village to the east those Colombians may not know of. That is where I wish for to go, por favor!"

"Sí, sí, un momento, Viejo. Does that road to the east lead anywhere *beyond* this village you speak of?"

"I do not know. I do not think so. But let me go, I beg of you!"

Captain Gringo let him go. Gaston, who'd joined them in time to hear most of it, sighed and said, "Eh bien. First things coming first, do you think we could blast through el Arbitrador and his thugs before those other thugs catch up with us?"

Captain Gringo said, "Not with one Maxim and the ammo left, with them dug in behind Celia's solid walls. There may be a better way. Let's try forward, into the Indian country ahead."

"Dick, I know you have a way with Indians. But have you forgotten there is a très formidable canyon to cross, with no bridge, that way?"

"We'll cross that bridge when we don't come to it. Let's at least get this mob off the fucking main drag!"

They did. And, as Gaston had foreseen, the Guaymi couldn't imagine what the hell he was leading an elephant through their woods for. So the same old jefe came out of the underbrush to ask.

Captain Gringo explained that the Colombian army was coming north, the way east led nowhere, and the way west was blocked. The jefe nodded soberly but pointed out that there just wasn't *any* way, north, and that all these odd-looking strangers were making his people nervous.

Captain Gringo said, "Look, if we can't do anything to stop the invasion, you and your people will be in the same sinking canoe with us all. So cut the bullshit about ancestral hunting grounds and help me hide this bunch, good, before you don't *have* anything to argue about!"

The Indians talked it over, decided they'd rather fight one bunch of strangers at a time, and even showed Captain Gringo to a clearing off the old trail where they might be safe, at least until the Colombians decided to secure the area with patrols.

Leaving most of his men and their charges there, Captain Gringo headed for another look at the ruined Indian bridge, with Gaston, Carlota, and Bombasto tagging along.

Captain Gringo didn't know why. He didn't need anyone to tell him he was wasting gray matter as he thoughtfully grabbed hold of a cable to test it, as if it *mattered* whether an old frayed rope dangling over churning white water far below was going to snap today or in a hundred years.

Gaston shook his head and said, "Merde alors, even if we had the time to restring the catwalk, we'd never get across with an elephant, or even *you*, you big moose!"

The tall American said, "We don't need to get our whole party across, dammit. Just one guy who can run would be enough. There are no Indians on the far side. It would be a safe, fairly short hike to Dutch Lansford and the others at Molina del Diablo, see?"

Gaston brightened and said, "Mais oui! With the extra machine guns and that adorable mountain mortar, Dutch could make short work of those bandits at Celia's farm!

No doubt they are there in the first place because Dutch disputed their passage across the bridge rather rudely. Mais, next question, how do we get even one of us across, hein?''

Bombasto frowned and said, "If I had a net to land in . . ." But Captain Gringo told him he was talking pretty silly and, since he was, Bombasto shut up.

Carlota stared at the sickeningly swaying rope and looked pretty sick herself as she said, "Deek, do you think you could manage to haul that line taut and keep it that way for me?"

He tugged experimentally, then said, "*You're* talking silly, too. Even a high-wire walker who was in practice would be a chump to try that, and you haven't been up in over three years. Besides, you told me you'd lost your nerve, Doll."

"I have. I do not know if I shall ever get it back. But if ever I intend to, can you think of a better time, Deek?"

He shook his head and said, "Honey, this is no circus. This is a war, and that's no net down there. Forget it. There's got to be a better way."

But there wasn't. So in the end they hauled the stronger-looking of the two ropes as tight as they could get it, and lashed it to trees as big as they could find, while Captain Gringo wrote a note to Dutch and cut Carlota the long pole she hoped to even the odds with. Then she kissed him adiós and, before she could change her mind, got up on the roughly braided rope, teetered a moment on her bare feet, and edged out over the abyss with the long pole held at waist level, as Gaston closed his eyes and muttered, "Tell me when it's over. I can't look."

Captain Gringo and Bombasto didn't want to look, either, but they did, as the erstwhile tightrope walker moved step by gingerly step along an improvised high wire that was not, in fact, too tight. A treacherous gust of breeze caught Carlota's robe and tried to pull her off, but managed only to expose her tattoos from the waist down as she leaned into it and then gracefully kept her balance by shifting the other way as it died.

But the wobble had frozen her in place, too far out to get back and not far enough across to matter. Captain Gringo quietly warned the others not to call out to her if they meant to go on living. So, after a sickening million years of hesitation, Carlota took another step, then another, and then something happened inside her, something they would never really understand, and Carlota was not only walking on, but walking like the big-top star she was!

Halfway across, she tossed away the pole and, as it fell end over end to the churning water below, turned and waved back to them, calling out across the gulf between them, "I have it back! I have it back!"

And then, as she turned to move on, as sure of herself as if she were strolling down a country lane, the old rope broke.

Carlota fell, and fell, a quarter mile or more, and if she screamed, nobody heard her, because they were screaming too!

And then she was gone. Only a swirling patch of pink foam moving rapidly downstream gave evidence she'd ever existed. Gaston sighed and murmured, "Eh bien, what could she have ever managed for an encore?" Then he ducked out of the way as Captain Gringo swung at him, missed, and growled, "God damn it, Gaston! That's not funny!"

Gaston said, "It was not meant to be. One often says odd things when one is trying not to cry. Are we going to beat each other up or draw straws to see who gets to try the remaining rope, Dick?"

Captain Gringo said, "Neither. She snapped the stronger-looking rope with her weight, and none of us are nearly as light as she was, even if we wanted to play sloth or something."

"Then we have no way of getting a message to Dutch and the others," Gaston said flatly. It was a statement, not a question.

But Captain Gringo turned to Bombasto and asked, "Can your cannon shoot across that gap?"

Bombasto nodded but said, "It would be suicide, without a net to land in on the other side."

"What about all those trees and bushes over there?"

"All right, *slow* suicide. Have you any idea how hard I land, even with the net to catch me?"

"Let's go back to where we left your cannon. We can dope out the details on the way."

They didn't. By the time they'd reached the circus gear, Bombasto had about convinced Captain Gringo that the whole idea was silly as well as probably fatal. But he called together a work gang to move the big cannon to the edge of the big canyon. There was no point in wheeling it down to where Carlota had died trying. The canyon was too wide at any point, if one listened to Bombasto. But the human cannonball cranked the big sheet-metal tube to maximum elevation as Captain Gringo ordered him to. Then he showed them how the powerful catapult springs worked, and, with extra hands on the cranks, the big dangerous fake gun was ready and waiting for a customer.

Then came the hard part. Bombasto stared down at the dirt at his feet as he said, "The spirit is willing, but the flesh is weak. I make no excuses for myself. I know it is our only chance. I know I will regret my cowardice when we are overrun by the invading army. But I just can't *do* it!"

Captain Gringo nodded and asked, "Will the springs loft a guy my size across, Bombasto?"

The human cannonball blanched and said, "That is not the question. What goes up must come down. *That* is the question. There is no *net* for anyone to land in on the far side, Captain Gringo!"

"You've told me that a lot lately. So what do I do, just climb inside and play the rest by ear?"

"My God, *no!* Unless you double up and hold on to your ankles, the shock can snap your spine. But I don't think a man your size can fit in the tube that way."

"What if I slide head first and brace my shoulders and the nape of my neck against the piston head?"

"I've never tried it. So I just can't say. Even if I can launch you without hurting you, how are you to *land,* dammit?"

"Let's eat this apple a bite at a time. Gaston, I'm counting on you, the boys, and that Maxim to hold this position till I can get back to you with more force. Can do?"

"Probably not. I'd rather see you manning that machine gun at my side than floating down the canyon after poor Carlota, Dick. Maybe we can hold here if we really have to."

"You'll have to, and you can't, if that Colombian column means business. Gimme a *boost,* dammit!"

So Gaston and Bombasto formed a cradle with their locked fingers and gave him a leg up into the mouth of the cannon. He knew as he slid down the tube that he wanted to be almost anywhere else. But he wasn't sure how one backed out of a cannon even if one wanted to.

His outstretched hands hit the bottom of the tube, and he was pleased to note that the piston was padded with leather, albeit almost as firm as wood. He got into position with his head and shoulders resting, if that was the word, against the bottom, with his boot heels up at an awkward angle. He yelled, "You may fire when ready, Bombasto! The blood's rushing to my fucking head!"

Bombasto released the catapult without a word of warning, dammit, and of course without the usual explosive charge that was simply for show. So Captain Gringo suddenly found himself way up in the middle of the air, flying ass-over-teakettle as blue sky and gut-wrenching views of the canyon below flashed across his eyes.

He remembered, now, that he'd forgotten to ask the human cannonball how the hell one was supposed to hit the net, balled up or flat. But there was no net ahead to catch him and he couldn't seem to control whether he was flying head first or feet first at the moment. So he just raised his knees, wrapped his arms around them, and hung on until suddenly pine boughs were whipping the shit out of him, a groping live oak clutched at his ass but managed only to rip open the seat of his pants, and then Mother Earth gave him a very sound spanking for being so silly. He bounced, rolled, bounced, and so on until, when he'd been punished enough, he stared groggy-eyed up through the forest canopy for a while, decided that nothing too serious seemed to be broken, after all, and groaned himself to his feet to get going to get help.

Dutch Lansford seemed delighted to see him, but kept asking stupid questions, like how on earth he'd crossed the canyon without a bridge, as Captain Gringo sat in the office at Molina del Diablo, sketching battle plans on a sketch pad the fake Jurado officer wasn't using these days. He told Dutch, "Never mind my recent adventures. *You're* about to have some pissers! Go get the men lined up. We're taking all but one machine-gun section to blow the bridge. And get the adelitas out of here in case this doesn't work. We're taking the mountain mortar and everything and everybody else that goes boom. Move it. I'll be finished here in a minute and you'd better be ready when I am!"

Dutch left. Captain Gringo finished the last tactical sketch meant for the last platoon leader and rose to rewire the magneto box, placing it on the desk with his back to the door. So when it opened again, he felt the breeze with his bare ass and growled, "What is it? I'm busy, dammit!"

A feminine voice replied, "You're exposing yourself, too. Do you wish for me to sew that rent in your pants, Deek?"

He looked over his shoulder to see the widow, Celia, blushing rather becomingly in the doorway. He said, "Haven't the time, thanks. What else can I do for you, Doll? If it takes longer than a kiss, I haven't got time for that, either."

She fluttered her lashes and said, "I'm still in mourning. I just wished for to ask when it may be safe to return to my estancia, Deek?"

He hesitated, then said, "Honey, unless you're talking about buried treasure or something, forget it. At the moment, a big band of outlaws occupies your old homestead as a new fort. We'll probably have to bust the place up some more to get through to Gaston and the others. Before you argue, if we don't blow them out through your roof tiles, a mess of Colombians with bigger guns will do so anyway, and meanwhile they'll be mopping up our friends the bandits have cut off from home."

Celia shrugged and said, "One can always rebuild, in a land where adobe, terra-cotta, and labor is so inexpensive. Your friend Dutch just told me outside that if all else fails, we on this side are to blow up the bridge and run for San José."

"He told you true. Don't worry about it. I'm leaving instructions with the ranking noncom left behind. So he'll know how to do it, if he has to do it."

"That box you are working on is for to detonate the explosives wired under the steel span, no?"

"Yes. But don't you or any of the other girls come anywheres near it. You can get a nasty shock if you don't know how to work the plunger, and I could get a nasty shock if anyone blew that bridge before they had to, with me on the other side!"

She said something about a needle and thread and left for the moment. A moment was all he needed to wire the situation to his liking. So, if she ever got back with her sewing kit, she missed him. He tore outside, whistled over the guerrilla he was leaving in charge here, and handed him a folded sheet of instructions regarding the blowing of bridges, with an added warning not even to *think* about it before he saw Colombian regulars on the other end of the span. Then he dogtrotted on to where Dutch had the main force lined up, with the mortar section at one end of the column, and called out, "At ease. Platoon leaders front and center to get your plans of action. Read 'em and weep. Then follow them to the letter unless I countermand 'em in the field. I don't expect to. This'll either go sweet and simple or we'll be in a hell of a mess. You all know the chain of command if I get hit. So let's get the fuck out of here. There's not much time to get in and out."

As the platoon leaders moved back into position, Captain Gringo joined Dutch at the head of the column and said, "Let's go. We won't need scouts out on point before we hit the first crossroads."

He led them quickstep to that point south of the bridge, put out his scouts, and didn't slow down on the route to Celia's occupied homestead.

The scouts reported that while the place was obviously crawling with armed desperados, El Arbitrador was, as Captain Gringo had hoped, a stupid bandit rather than a smart guerrilla, so there was no picket line in the woods around the cleared field of fire.

Captain Gringo didn't have to give many orders as the platoon leaders followed his instructions and spread out their skirmish lines along the tree line. Dutch whistled the mortar crew forward, gave them the range figures, and, as they elevated and loaded the brass barrel, asked Captain Gringo when he wanted them to fire. The tall American didn't turn from his view of the farm-building cluster as he watched it through the sights of a fully loaded Maxim and growled, "Now."

So, a few moments later, red roof tiles and bloody scraps of rag and human flesh were rising skyward as mortar round after mortar round crumped right on target. As survivors dived out doors and windows, Captain Gringo pulled the Maxim off its tripod, stood up with it braced on one hip, and charged forward across the open ground, hosing death ahead of him as, from the tree line to either side, his guerrillas advanced in a deadly walking-fire skirmish line.

Meanwhile, on the far side of all this death and destruction, advance units of the invading Colombian army had reached the crossroads leading to Celia's, or nowhere much, or Gaston's position in the forest to the north, or back home where they belonged. The choice was theirs.

The field-grade officer in command had been about to order patrols into the Indian country to the north, where Gaston's guerrillas, the stranded circus folk, and the Indians were braced with their backs to the canyon. But as all hell seemed to be breaking loose to the *west,* the Colombian ordered his cavalry screen down that road and followed with his infantry and battery of field guns. It did not turn out to be such a wise move, in the end.

The Colombian cavalry screen got in trouble first. As professionals and not mere butchers at heart, the saber-swinging cavalry troopers slapped all but a few wise asses with the flats of their blades as the panic-stricken refugees dashed through their formation in a headlong flight from the sounds of battle to the west. A bright as well as humanitarian Colombian officer shouted, "Into the *woods,* you idiots! Keep this road cleared if you want to enjoy the next sunset!"

Most obeyed. But clearing the road had broken the Colombian formation, and so, when El Arbitrador's survivors hit them next—and only the toughest survived—the results were a dusty chaos, with the cavalry commander's saddle empty before he could give any sensible orders and El Arbitrador's skull empty soon after, when a cursing Colombian cavalry trooper blew his brains out before *he* could call a retreat to his own men.

They wouldn't have retreated in any case, now. They were taking fire from both sides now, and the fire from Captain Gringo's three machine guns and massed Krags was awesome. So they bulled on down the road, pushing the Colombian cavalry ahead of them whether they wanted to go that way or not, until, as plunging machine-gun fire began to empty even more saddles, they decided they sure *wanted* to!

As the milling mob of friend and foe came down the dust-blurred road at the Colombian commander and his infantry, he blinked, gulped, and told his riflemen to for chrissake spread out and take cover. So they did, just in time to lay withering fire into what was left of the big bandit gang while the few cavalrymen left rode through them, dismounted, and flopped down beside the infantry with their cavalry carbines, still wondering what in the *hell* they'd run into. They'd been assured in Panama City that the cowardly Costa Ricans wouldn't offer much resistance. Someone must have been confused, no?

As Captain Gringo's skirmish line moved close enough to start taking casualties from dug-in rifles, they of course hit the dirt, too. Captain Gringo joined them there, cursing as he cradled his hot Maxim, looking for a target ahead, but spotting nothing but the dead or dying under a hanging pall of dust and gunsmoke.

He still had to get through to Gaston and the others. But now he was up against the real thing. Trained regulars didn't cut and run just because it was getting noisy all of a sudden. Good soldiers retreated only when they had a damned good reason, and all the reasons he had with him were fewer riflemen, the machine guns with nothing to aim at unless the Colombians were dumb enough to break cover, and the pisspot little mortar.

So when Dutch crawled over to him, asking what next, Captain Gringo said, "Let's give 'em some mortar rounds for luck."

Dutch frowned and asked, "Whose luck are we talking about? If they range on our one and only gun position . . ."

"God damn it, Dutch *do* it!"

So Dutch moved back to the mortar crew, hoping very much that the army unit they'd run into hadn't brought along its own heavy weapons.

The Colombians not only had, but at the moment were elevating all four field guns of the battery, lined up on the crossroads near Gaston as they estimated the range. The battery commander had of course thought to send a patrol up the blind alley trail running into the woods from his right flank. But the Indians, at Gaston's suggestion, had of course made sure no Colombian scouts returned to report anything but peace and tranquillity as the small but deadly Frenchman made plans of his own.

As an old artilleryman, Gaston was ranging by ear, too, as he led his own guerrillas and Guaymi volunteers through the thick woods to flank the Colombian battery. He wasn't as husky as Captain Gringo. So when he got into position with a clear field of flanking fire ahead of him, Gaston simply braced the Maxim his taller friend had left behind across a fallen log and proceeded to shoot the liver and lights out of the enemy artillerymen. His riflemen gleefully took care of the few he missed.

By the time Gaston had secured the area, Captain Gringo's first mortar rounds were landing all along the defense line of the now very worried Colombian infantry and surviving cavalry to the west.

Gaston cocked an ear and told the hitherto useless human cannonball, Bombasto, "Voilà! If our young friend is lobbing those très familiar if primitive mortar rounds on anyone, they can't be friends of ours. I make the range one and one-half kilometers. Allow me to show you how one fires a *real* cannon!"

With the help of Bombasto and some other willing pupils, Gaston loaded all four field guns, checked the elevation again, and told everyone holding a lanyard, "Fire!"

Then, even as the first four rounds were screaming toward the Colombian positions between him and Captain Gringo, Gaston shouted, "Reload and prepare to fire again, dammit. You, Frutos, move your otherwise tedious riflemen out to form a dug-in screen, hein? We may have to fight for the custody of these adorable orphans if I have the elevation wrong!"

They didn't. Actually, Gaston's blind ranging, estimated safely short to avoid hitting the wrong people, landed behind, not right on, the Colombian defense line. But close enough to literally scare the shit out of them as their ears rang and the ground rolled in jellylike waves under them. Some leaped up, running blindly from the shell fire behind them into the deadly rifle and machine-gun fire waiting for them to break cover. Most, of course, were too well trained to panic. But they still had to get the hell out of there. So they did so the smart way, slipping south like melon seeds in a too-tight squeeze until it was safe to stand up and run due south, toward a border that most sincerely now believed they never should have crossed in the first place.

Their commander didn't order anyone to try to get back their big guns. He was no dope. It was obvious enough that when one's own guns are bombarding one, they've been captured by somebody tougher than the ones you *left* them with!

Thus, within an hour, Captain Gringo's scouts had made contact with Gaston's scouts, and since nobody but a few easily disposed of wounded now lay between them, Captain Gringo and Gaston got to shake hands in the middle of some thoroughly shot-up real estate that now seemed to belong to Costa Rica after all.

Gaston said, "Don't tell me how you made it. I hate tall stories. Do we dig in here, or will you listen to your elders for a change and get us all across that fucking bridge?"

Captain Gringo laughed and said, "I don't think they'll be back. But if they come at all, this is no place to stand off a no-doubt thoroughly pissed-off army. Let's get *everybody* across the canyon and see what happens next."

Doing so was easier said than done. But with even the Indians helping now, they finally got the elephant, circus gear, and stranded circus freaks headed the right way. One Guaymi squaw insisted on carrying the pretty little human caterpillar like a baby and couldn't understand why the cute little thing insisted she enjoyed circus life more than she'd probably enjoy being some kind of Indian goddess. The Indians didn't invite the fat lady to join their tribe. They knew they'd never be able to feed her.

It seemed to take forever, but the sun was still up there, just, as Captain Gringo led the head of the column out onto the bridge at Molina del Diablo. On the far side, the sergeant he'd left in command waved with obvious relief. Some of the adelitas, including the tall black Nina Brea and the once-sulky little Angelica, could do better than that by walking out on the span, holding hands, to meet him. He was sort of looking forward to sunset now.

Then, with even the poor dumb elephant out on the span above the abyss, there was a deafening explosion, the shock waves shook the bridge under them, and everyone but Captain Gringo thought they'd been killed.

He knew better. So he ran forward, past his adelitas, past the other bewildered guerrillas and adelitas, toward the column of smoke mushrooming up through the shattered roof of the military command post.

Inside, things were a hell of a mess. In the swirling sunset-illuminated haze he saw that his desk and the magneto box he'd placed on it no longer existed. The tile floor was cratered where they'd been. The windows as well as the roof had been blown out, of course. But what looked at first like a fat paper doll, pasted to one wall and still sort of recognizable as Celia, slowly slid down the blasted plaster like wet paint. Mostly red.

Gonzalez and too many of the others crowded in through what was left of the door, all shouting at once. So Captain Gringo ordered everyone but Gaston and Dutch back out for now, and even they asked too many questions at once. So he yelled at them to shut up, and when they did, he said, "I left instructions with Gonzalez to rewire the magneto box, very carefully, if the time ever came to blow that bridge. Then I booby-trapped the plunger with leftover dynamite tucked in the one desk drawer I could lock. I didn't bother to tell anyone but Gonzalez. I wanted it to be a surprise, and it must have been, when our Jurado playmate tried to kill us all on the bridge just now."

Gaston stared soberly at what was left of Celia, now sort of a puddle against the baseboard, and said, "Correct me if I am wrong. But was not that the dress the pretty widow, Celia, was wearing the last time I admired her figure?''

Captain Gringo nodded grimly and said, ''She wasn't a she. She was a skinny *he,* sort of. Getting your balls cut off when you're young enough leaves you sort of effeminate-looking. But there was nothing womanly about the cocksucker. He probably didn't even suck cock. He was a dedicated fanatic. He knew from the moment we met him that he owed us for what we'd done to his Jurado pals. So he was just waiting for his chance to kill as many of us as he could, once we'd stopped his *Colombian* enemies.''

Gaston frowned thoughtfully and said, ''Merde alors, she, I mean it, certainly had *me* fooled! What tipped you off, Dick? Have you been reaching under skirts très sneaky again?''

Captain Gringo smiled thinly and said, ''No. He was counting on the fact that nobody but a total louse would make a real pass at a recent widow. But the widow story rubbed me a little wrong from the beginning. I kept hoping I was wrong. For one thing, as a real woman, the son of a bitch wasn't bad-looking.''

He got out a claro, lit it, and continued, ''As you'll remember, our friend's story when we apparently rescued him was that he had hidden up the chimney while bad banditos robbed the place and moved on. That story's probably true, but it left out a few details. Before those outlaws showed up, a band of Jurados fleeing the Colombian army hit the place first, killing the real farmers and probably the real Celia, if that was even her name. Then, as they were moving on, this way, they got ambushed good among the trees. Our so-called Celia was the only Jurado who made it back alive to the house. The others who killed them were long gone.''

Gaston brightened and said, ''Oui, we wondered how anyone could pick off so many men at that range. Our adorable Celia, still wearing its Jurado uniform, hid up the chimney while Pablo looted the place and rode on. Then it got back down, changed its no-doubt uniform for a dress, really the property of the dead farm wife, and . . . But the *hair*, Dick."

Captain Gringo pointed at the mess at their feet with a boot tip and asked, "What hair?" So Gaston slapped a palm against his own forehead and replied, "Of course, the farmer's wife no doubt had a wig to remind her of her younger days when she went to church, hein? Now that I think back, our Celia was wearing *boots* as well as a wig, non?"

Captain Gringo said, "Boots were barely possible, for a campesina who rode a lot instead of going barefoot like most countrywomen this far south. I was more worried about her empty shotgun. She said she'd been holding off bandits with a shotgun after all the *men* in the place had been picked off. Again, possible, when you include the last mad dash up the chimney after running out of shotgun shells. But I did sort of wonder how come she'd been so *lucky*, with everyone else exchanging long-range rifle fire. Okay, call me a horny rascal who likes to think pretty girls are really pretty girls. Or call me too polite to ask a recent widow to lift her skirts and then explain *why*, if I'd been wrong. I went along with Celia's gag, whatever his name was, once I saw that whatever it was wasn't heavily armed and seemed to be acting friendly."

He grinned sheepishly and added, "I was planning to make sure, the fun way, once we got back. I was hoping Celia was a real widow who might be ready to be consoled. But just in case she, it, or anybody else we had to leave on this side of the bridge was a sneak, I made sure *nobody* was about to blow that bridge except the one guy I trusted."

Dutch whistled thoughtfully and said, "Remind me never to disobey an order from you, Dick. But how did you know you could trust *Gonzalez?* We hardly know the guy."

Captain Gringo looked at Gaston and asked, "You want to tell him, or shall I?"

Gaston turned to Dutch and said, "I have a Private

Gonzalez under *my* command, too. He is the son of the Sergeant Gonzalez Dick left in command *here*.''

Dutch laughed and said, ''Jesus, don't you guys ever take chances?''

Captain Gringo said, ''Soldiers aren't paid to take chances they don't have to. We'd better get those captured field guns over on this side and sandbagged into position, poco tiempo, just in case the Colombians feel like taking more chances I hope to convince them they don't really have to.''

As darkness fell, Captain Gringo put pickets on the far side of the bridge, told the adelitas, circus folk, and the men he'd marched the asses off that day to go eat supper, screw, or whatever, as long as they kept out of the way. Then, with fresher guerrillas and the elephant's help, he proceeded to set up more-imposing defenses north of the bridge.

He masked the captured artillery, of course, but left Bombasto's big fake cannon vaguely visible behind a lower wall of sandbags and branches. It wouldn't shoot worth a damn, but that could be hard to tell from a distance once the imposing red ''cannon'' had been made even more imposing by a coat of khaki-colored 'dobe. He set up machine-gun nests to crossfire anything trying to cross the span. Then, having done all he could for now, he went to the nearest cook fire, wolfed down some tortillas and coffee, then went looking for his adelitas to see if they'd really meant that warm welcome home.

They were in the room assigned to them inside the garrison walls. And they were warm indeed at the moment. Neither looked up from what she was doing as he stood in the doorway, bemused.

Watching a willowy black girl and a chunky mestiza going sixty-nine across the bunk was sort of stimulating, but he couldn't see just how *he'd* fit in, before all three of them had taken one long hot bath. So he left them moaning and groaning words of endearment up each other's cunts for the moment, now that he saw there was time to enjoy a relaxed smoke or, hell, a good night's sleep *alone* for a change.

As he passed another doorway he heard heartbroken sobs coming from the other side. He knocked gently and, when a sweet sad voice called out, "Entrada!" he stepped into the dimly candlelit room to find the human caterpillar sobbing alone on the army cot provided for her.

He smiled down at her and said, "I'm sorry. It was stupid of them to leave you alone. I'll post one of the adelitas to stay with you and, uh, help you get about. Is there anything I can do for you before I go to fetch her?"

The limbless girl shook her head and said, "I do not wish for any company, gracias. I can move about quite well, in my own grotesque way. That is for why they call me a human caterpillar, see?"

"Sorry. Missed your act, Señorita . . . ?"

"I am called Ana, by my few friends. Does it surprise you a monster has friends at all?"

He grimaced and said, "You're not a monster. You're a pretty girl who got a bad break, Ana. I am called Dick. Now that that's settled, what are you crying about if there's nothing you want?"

She sobbed as she said, "It is not fair! Those siamese twins have already found new lovers. *Two* of them! It's disgusting for four people to go to bed together, don't you agree?"

He suppressed a laugh and said, "I don't see how *else* siamese twins would work it, unless one guy was awfully ambitious, and the bed would still be a little crowded, so what the hell."

The human caterpillar fluttered her eyelashes suggestively and said, "There is only one woman in this bed, Deek."

He gasped in surprise and couldn't answer, because, actually, all he saw was what looked like a terrycloth sack with a woman's head sticking out of it. But it wouldn't have been at all polite to say so.

She said bitterly, "Never mind. I know all too well that look in a man's eyes. You may go now. I assure you I shall not attack you."

He laughed despite himself, and then, noting the pain in her big beautiful eyes, said quickly, "It's not that I don't find you attractive, Ana. It's just that... Aw, hell, what kind of a guy do you take me for?"

She looked away, saying, "A handsome one. I have never had a really handsome man. Even the few clowns who have taken pity on me were only, in the end, clowns."

"Jesus, you mean, people like you..."

"Are not freaks people too?" she replied bitterly. Then she blushed as she added softly, "It is worse when one has not even hands for to relieve the tension, alone at night in the endless dark, while all about you, even the reptile girl and the two-headed boy, are having sex."

He must have looked as shocked as he felt. For she said, "Forgive me. I have not had the social advantages for to learn the proper way to speak of such matters. I can see I have spoken too much about problems that are beyond a normal person's concern or understanding. You had better go now. I feel the need for to cry some more."

He sat on the edge of her bunk and placed a gentle hand on her shoulder, if she had a shoulder; it was hard to tell.

He said, "I'm trying to understand, Ana. It's not my fault, any more than it's yours, that we were born a bit different."

"Do not lecture me!" she snapped, adding, "God, if you knew how tired we are of hearing pious platitudes from you damned normals! We do not need to be told we are freaks who must learn to live with it. We need people who can *help* us live with it!"

He nodded and said, "So ask, Ana."

She said, "I did. What do you expect a woman to say, that she is going loco en la cabeza because she has not enjoyed an orgasm in over a year? Even nuns were born with *hands,* God damn them! I am, as you see, dependent on the kindness of others! You took pity on the tattooed lady. Why can't you feel pity for me? Am I really that repulsive?''

He frowned and asked, ''Who's been speaking ill of the dead? Carlota died a star. Let's not be spreading gossip about her, eh?''

The pretty little freak said, ''Pooh, do you think I would be speaking so boldly if Carlota herself had not boasted of her night with you? We freaks, I fear, tend to boast overmuch of our conquests, since we have so few to boast of.''

He didn't answer. He just sat there feeling the back of his neck turn red until Ana sighed and added, ''She said you were a most virile but most gentle lover. Won't you, *can't* you, show me what she meant?''

He said, ''I know what it feels like to be hard up, even with hands to keep you company in bed. But I don't think I'd be *able* to, Ana. It's not that I find you ugly. It's just that, well, I've never molested children up to now and . . .''

''Help me out of this sack and I'll show you who's a child!'' she cut in, adding, ''I have the important parts, at least, of a normal woman. Furthermore, I do not have to worry about getting in trouble like some foolish peon girl you would find more desirable might. When I was still too young to worry about such matters, a family doctor made sure I could never get pregnant, lest I be raped in my helpless condition.''

Then she almost spat as she continued, ''God, if only that would *happen* once in a while! But you damned men are all alike. Nobody has ever wished for to rape me, and most, like you, refuse when I *beg* for it!''

He could see she was really hurting. He knew all too well what it felt like to be sexually frustrated. So he said, ''Look, I'll snuff out the candle and maybe, ah, help you out with my hand, okay?''

She said, ''Fuck the candle! Just do *something,* poco

tiempo! I am gushing with desire and I God damn it can't even play with myself!''

He said, ''Okay, okay, don't scream.'' Then he took a deep breath and gingerly reached for the bottom of the sack. What he felt inside felt strange indeed. Ana moaned as she said, ''Not through that rough toweling, dammit! Help me out of this costume and do it *right,* por favor!''

He didn't think he wanted to, but he did. He unfastened the drawstring of her so-called costume and gingerly bared her tiny armless shoulders as she helped by wriggling out of it like a butterfly emerging from a fuzzy cocoon. But as she moved on the bedding in her grotesque caterpillar way, she sure looked a lot more womanly than anything he'd ever seen come out of a cocoon before!

She rolled over on her back, not spreading her thighs, since she had none, but thrusting her oddly narrow pelvis up to him, with her small firm breasts flushed with desire and her exposed and fully mature vaginal opening glistening pink and wet in the candlelight. The lids of her lovely eyes were closed as she pleaded, ''Do it, do it, *do* it!''

He repressed a shudder, leaned down, and kissed her as he took her armless body in one arm and caressed her limbless but otherwise perfectly formed torso with his free hand.

Ana pleaded, with her warm lips against his, ''Don't tease me, please. Please make me *come,* for God's sake! I have not come in over a year!''

He cupped her privates in his free hand, nestled her aroused and surprisingly large clit between two love-slicked fingers, and proceeded to jerk her off as she, in turn, responded with the damnedest movements of her legless pelvis. She gasped as she cried, ''Inside! Inside! I have to have something for to grip down on as I come!''

So he slid the two fingers in her, massaging her clit with his palm, and when that didn't seem enough, he worked a third, then a fourth, up into her desperate love box.

She damn near cracked his knuckles when she came. She went limp, an easy thing for a human caterpillar to do, and sighed. "Oh, thank you, thank you, thank you! Would you make it happen again?"

He started playing with her some more. She sighed and said, "Don't you have anything nicer than your *hand* for me, Deek?"

As a matter of fact, he was getting an erection that was probably never going to forgive him if he passed on this. He even tried to tell his head that it ought to seriously consider going further. But his head kept telling him not to be such a shit. So he kissed her to shut her up as he continued to give her a helping hand.

For by the same inner workings of the mind that make most wife beaters afraid to fight grown men, a naturally dominant male who's *not* afraid of other men finds it hard to mistreat women, even when they're asking for it.

Ana was more than asking, she was begging him to take off his damned duds and put it to her dog, or in this case caterpillar, style by the time he'd brought her to climax again, and his own throbbing caterpillar was obviously in favor of the idea, too. But the few times a lady had talked him into bondage he'd felt silly instead of stimulated because he didn't *want* his sex partner helpless. He liked it better when a woman perfectly capable of kicking him in the crotch and scratching his eyes out preferred to *offer* sweet and willing submission instead of having no choice.

Hence, it wasn't the fact that Ana was crippled that repelled him even as her otherwise womanly body attracted him. It was knowing that he could do anything he wanted to her, whether she wanted him to or not, that made him feel guilty about the little he was doing for her.

She suddenly went into convulsions, or perhaps an unusually good orgasm, and then she sort of fainted. But her face was too red and she was crying too much to be unconscious. He didn't ask her what was the matter as he caressed her down from the heights. He could see how, from her point of view, he was being cruel to her. He didn't want to be cruel, but Jesus, could he really go all the way and not feel like a shit later? Maybe if he blew out

the candle . . . He sure as hell couldn't *look* at their
mismatched bodies going at it hot and heavy and . . . How
the hell was a guy supposed to *position* himself with a
human caterpillar?

He gave her a friendly reassuring pat and rose to snuff
the candle. As the room was plunged in darkness, Ana
sobbed and said, "Oh, thank you, Deek. I feel so
embarrassed now, but I did not know how to tell you to put
out the light, after saying all those wild and wicked things
to you."

He rejoined her on the cot and put a comforting brotherly hand on her, in a more brotherly place, as he said
quietly, "Lots of things we say or even do when we're
excited don't sound so great once we calm down."

She sobbed in the darkness. "I know. Oh, what must
you think of me now?"

"I think you're a beautiful woman who got a little
carried away by passion. Are you, ah, feeling calmer
now?"

There was a long moment of silence. Then Ana murmured,
"It would not be fair to refuse you *now!* But please be
gentle and do not be hurt if I fail to respond, at least at
first, eh?"

He said, "I've got a better idea. Suppose we put your,
ah, costume back on and let you get some sleep. You've
had enough excitement for one day."

As he began to help her back into her pathetic terrycloth
sack, Ana continued to sob. "Oh, you are so understanding of a woman's feelings. Why do we have such fickle
feelings, Deek?"

"Beats me. I've never been a woman. But I know better
than to argue with 'em. Here we are. Want me to tie the
drawstring or leave it loose?"

"Tie it, por favor. I can't. Are you angry with me,
Deek?"

"Did I act like I was angry with you just now?"

"No, you acted like an angel of mercy, and I fear I am
being cruel. If you had wanted to, you could have done

anything you wanted to me, and, in God's truth, I probably would have enjoyed it. But now that the tension is relieved . . . Perhaps if we waited a bit, I could get back in the mood.''

He bent down in the dark, kissed her forehead, and said, "Go to sleep. You know you're fighting to stay awake right now."

"Si, but how will *you* ever get to sleep now?"

He answered her dumb question with another dumb kiss and got up to get the hell out of there, muttering under his breath, "It won't be easy. I'm either a hell of a swell guy or a stupid sissy. Some night when I'm alone and hard up in a strange town, I'll probably know which I was tonight."

In the morning Captain Gringo ordered the circus folk, refugees, adelitas, and other noncombatants evacuated to the north. He told the weeping and wailing adelitas they could stop and make camp just outside artillery range if they promised to behave. He told Bombasto he had to leave his big tin cannon behind but that he'd get it back when the war was over, unless Costa Rica lost.

While he was at it, he rummaged through the circus gear to see if the runaway management had left behind any other props he might be able to use. Nothing they had looked at all like a weapon. But at least a rather spiffy bandmaster's uniform provided him with a new pair of pants. They fit okay and everyone admired the gold stripes down the light blue legs.

After that the day got sort of boring.

Once the noncombatants were gone and all that could be done to beef up the defenses had been done, there was nothing to do and nobody to screw. So they just got to wait, then wait some more until, late in the afternoon, a scout ran across the bridge to report dust, a lot of dust, coming at them from the southeast.

Captain Gringo sent him back to bring in the outposts

across the canyon. There were no other orders to give. So he didn't give any. His men were dug in, his artillery was ranged, so what the fuck was keeping those jerk-off Colombians he'd been waiting for all day?

The first thing they spotted coming at them across the bridge was a civilian carriage, a rather spiffy one, drawn by a matched team of high-stepping but now pretty dusty Spanish mules. The closed carriage was dusty too, as was the well-dressed coachman who reined in as directed on the safe side of the bridge and called down, "A Colombian column is right behind us, Señores! Thank God we find you here! These mules are about to give out, and should they catch us now . . ."

Captain Gringo cut in, "They won't. Wheel that carriage into that garrison yard over there and water the poor brutes. You and your passengers can take shelter inside the walls until you're ready to go on. But stay the hell out of our way till you do."

The coachman blessed him and drove on. Dutch Lansford, walking over in time to catch the last of the exchange, asked, "Want me to search 'em, Dick? A carriage that size could carry all sorts of goodies."

"If they were on the other side, they wouldn't have driven over to this side in such a hurry. They probably do have valuables on 'em. But we've put all the bandits around here out of business. So let's not go into the business ourselves. There's nothing they can steal in that empty shell. So forget 'em unless they do something dumb. Is Gaston all set up?"

"Yeah, that's what he sent me to tell you. He's got the mortar ranged on the far bridge ramp, with the bigger guns set to lay a barrage for them to run back through."

"That sounds like Gaston. Heads up, I see a white flag waving at us across the canyon now. Get back to your riflemen and stick to the plan. I'll see what the cocksuckers want."

He'd expected a parley, first. So he picked up his own preprepared parley flag and walked out on the bridge, feeling sort of bull's-eye as well as bullshit. Nobody shot at him from across the canyon. So the other coming out to meet him had to be offering terms. That seemed more reasonable than anything else they'd done, so far.

The officer from the other side was a first lieutenant they probably figured they could spare. He was trying not to look as scared as he had to be, if he had any brains at all. Captain Gringo lowered his own parley flag to his side, leaned against the guardrail, and said, "Buenas tardes, Lieutenant. What does your Colonel Maldonado have in mind?"

The Colombian blinked in surprise and asked, "Who told you he was our commander, Señor . . . ?"

"Walker. Captain Walker. Maldonado and I have bumped noses before. He's a good soldado. I hope he's still a sensible one. Because you guys are in a lot of trouble if you don't get the fuck back across the border before it's too late."

The enemy officer was staring thoughtfully past Captain Gringo. Captain Gringo wanted him to. He said conversationally, "It gets worse. This bridge is wired. You can see the charges if you look over the side."

The Colombian sniffed and said, "I will take your word for that. I see you have our captured guns elevated on our present positions, too."

"Don't worry, Lieutenant. We won't fire unless you force us to. By the way, my machine guns are zeroed on this bridge, too. Don't want to blow it if we don't have to. So the question before the house is, do you think we'll have to?"

"We of course wish for to avoid useless bloodshed. My side offers you full honors of war and no hindrance should you choose to evacuate Molina del Diablo peacefully."

Captain Gringo grinned and said, "Great minds must run in the same channels. I was about to offer you the same terms. I may as well be frank with you, Lieutenant. I don't have the reenforcements they're sending me just yet. So I won't be in a position to chase you, if you head for the border just about now. In a day or so, I'm afraid I won't be able to act so nice. Hasn't anybody ever told you it makes people mad when you jump borders?''

"We were only in hot pursuit of rebels and bandits, Captain Walker. By the way, are not those pants U.S. Marine issue?"

"Never mind about my pants. We both know all the rebels and bandits around here are out of business for keeps. So what's keeping *you* here, if it's not a land grab?''

"Such matters are not for us junior officers to decide. What if we made a deal about this canyon? It would form an obvious natural boundary between Panama and Costa Rica, no?''

"No. The map says the border's over a day's march to the south. So if I were in your boots, that's where I'd march 'em, before it's too late.''

The Colombian didn't like the idea at all. So to cut the bullshit a bit Captain Gringo lit a smoke, the agreed-on signal, and Dutch Lansford stood up behind his sandbags near the north end of the bridge to call out, in English, "What's the story, Major? What do the greasers want?"

Captain Gringo turned in mock anger to roar, "God damn it, Captain, I told you guys to stay out of sight! You know our orders, damn your eyes!"

So Dutch, wearing the circus bandmaster's dark blue tunic and white peaked cap, dropped out of sight. Then he started crawling to find another place along the line where he could show them a flash of white hat across the canyon.

The Colombian officer's face was a study in poker bluff as he said, in a desperately casual tone, "I thought you said you were only a captain.''

Captain Gringo shrugged and said, "What can I tell you? You know most guerrillas don't know one rank from another.''

"With all due respect, that did not look like a *guerrilla* just now! It looked, correct me if I am wrong, like a Yanqui Marine officer!''

Captain Gringo laughed, looked a little shifty-eyed, and said, "Don't be silly. What would the U.S. Marines be doing in a place like this? You know how fond Tío Sam is of your ruling junta."

"I do indeed. I was *wondering* where you got that big howitzer you, forgive me, might have camouflaged a little better."

"Oh, that? Hell, that's not a real gun. It's just something some circus people left behind, see?"

"I see more, perhaps, than you wish me to," the Colombian said stiffly. Then, since few people can resist showing off how much smarter than you they are, he added with a knowing crooked grin, "Tell your Costa Rican friends it won't work, Yanqui. Did you really think we'd be dumb enough to offer the United States Marines, and, of course, Yanqui gunboats, such a good excuse for gunboat diplomacy?"

"I don't know what you're talking about, Lieutenant. I assure you there's not a United States Marine or gunboat within a hundred miles of here. The reenforcements I mentioned are just plain old Costa Rican troops, see?"

"I just told you how well I can see, you Yanqui cardsharp! So now, if you will forgive me, I must get back to my command post to report this most revolting development!"

They saluted each other as if they were each snapping shit off their fingers. Then they turned their backs on each other to vacate the bridge span.

Within the hour, a dust cloud on the far side of the canyon was drifting southeast. Captain Gringo sent scouts across to make sure anyway. The first runner back confirmed that it was a full evacuation. So Captain Gringo grinned at Gaston and Dutch and said, "You see? If I'd *told* them such a crazy story they'd have never bought it in a million years. But suspicious people can find burglars under every bed, when you leave it to them to figure out. I'd better check out the passengers in that carriage before we send them on their way."

He headed for the garrison. Before he got there a dusty uniformed rider came in from the north with a message from Colonel Vegas. Captain Gringo opened the sealed envelope, read it, and called Gaston over. He said, "The old man must have worms or something. He's ordering me to report in person on the situation here."

Gaston shrugged and said, "Eh bien, he'll probably pin a medal on you or, better yet, give us a bonus, when you tell him what a sweet situation it is. We saved his bridge. We probably saved him a war. Go take a bow. I can handle things here until you can send someone to relieve us, hein?"

Captain Gringo nodded and said, "I could use a hot bath, and the sooner they get the good news the sooner we'll *all* be out of this grubby place. Okay, take over, Gaston. I'll see if there's room in that carriage for me. I sure as shit don't want to *walk* back to San José."

He went to the garrison to find the coachman rehitching the now watered and rested team to the carriage. Its one and only passenger was just stepping out from the shade, as if ready to leave. She wore expensive black silk and lace to go with her expensive carriage. Better yet, she was just plain lovely. Her cameo features were framed by soft chestnut curls and old Spanish lace. A tiny gold cross nestled in the cleavage above her low-cut bodice. But from the way she smiled up at him he doubted that she was any more religious than he was. So he smiled back the same way and told her, "I need a lift to San José, Señorita. Could I impose on you, if you're going that far?"

She held out a manicured hand and replied in a pleasant contralto, "I would be most happy to have company on an otherwise most tedious journey, Señor. As for how far I wish to go with you, we can discuss that along the way, no?"

So he took her hand and put another, friendlier one on her bottom to boost her. She didn't seem annoyed, even when his hand slipped a bit. So *he* felt much less annoyed, now, about the frustrations of the previous night. Because on the rare occasions when a mere male got *this* lucky, he was sure to need plenty of ammunition to defend the honor of his sex.